I0720828

FURIES' DAUGHTERS
Four Feisty Women

FURIES' DAUGHTERS
Four Feisty Women

Stories by
Gary Carr

Lightwood Press

Book design: Rachel Stern
Editor: Laura Ornella
FIRST EDITION, Published by Lightwood Press
Lightwoodpress.com

ISBN 978-1-7354410-8-5

The Ongoing Life of Margo Macomber originally appeared in History Through Fiction
magazine (Minneapolis). historythroughfiction.com
Other books by Gary Carr
The Girl Who Founded Nebraska and Other Stories
The Left Side of Paradise: The Screenwriting of John Howard Lawson

For Kathy, who is always there.

TABLE OF CONTENTS

PREFACE

Strong women fascinate me; women who use their talent and wits to claim their place in a patriarchal society. Eleanor Roosevelt, Marie Curie, Billy Jean King. Many more have been overlooked by history, like computer pioneer Grace Hopper, like Hollywood star Hedy Lamarr, who developed the system that led to technologies like Wi-Fi and Bluetooth, like Margaret Knight, who invented the paper bag

The four stories in this book present four feisty women. Jenny Gets Her Wheels On comes from what I know about theater, comedy performers, and life.

The Girl with the Topaz Ring began as a fourteen-month-long series in a California newsletter, The Clayton Valley Villager.

The Ongoing Life of Margo Macomber has been published previously in History Through Fiction magazine. It builds on what might have happened to Margo Macomber immediately after the shooting of her husband in Ernest Hemingway's short story, The Short Happy Life of Francis Macomber. I owe the historical references at the end to Rachel Maddow's book, Prequel.

Thea and Fritz: Berlin 1931–1933 traces three years in the lives of Germany's most famous screenwriter/director teams just before Hitler came into power. Thea von Harbou (von HAR-boo) and Fritz Lang are responsible for two films ranked in every critic's Top 100 — *Metropolis* and *M*, the latter, featuring Peter Lorre in his film debut. The scene in which Joseph Goebbels questions Lang comes from my 1972 interview with Lang himself. Lang fled Germany for Hollywood and became a major influence on psychological drama and film noir. Von Harbou stayed in Germany and…well, you'll have to read it.

Gary Carr

Gunter, Texas

JENNY GETS HER WHEELS ON

The tall stand-up comic shuffled off the stage. He left the microphone extended to its full height. His set did not go well.

The audience grumbled and rattled the ice in their glasses, a signal that they needed refills. The M.C. scurried into the spotlight and lowered the mic as far down as it would go. A man in the half-empty room muttered, "What's next, a chimp?"

"Now, a new face, and you're gonna love her," the M.C. responded. "Ladies and gentlemen, put your hands together for a very funny lady, Jenny Corraggio."

The half-hearted applause dissipated as Jenny Corraggio wheeled herself to the mic. She sat in a wheelchair designed for competition sports. "What is this, wheelchair basketball?" cracked the same guy. His date shushed him.

Jenny grabbed the mic.

"How do you like my wheels? Yeah, wheelchair-bound. Leaps and bounds. But it's the life…" She leaned into the mic and whispered seductively, "…of a low riderrrrrrr. "Funny the way people react when you're in a wheelchair. The other day, I was waiting for the light at a crosswalk. A lady with a little boy comes up to me and says, 'Can Trevor sit on your lap and ride across the street with you?' 'Sure,' I say, 'I love having a man between my legs.' She called me a pervert. I called her a bitch. Just another day in paradise. I wasn't always like this, ya know. I was a budding actor. Or actress, for you old farts over fifty. We had faces then. That's a reference for all you film buffs… Come on, this is L.A. There's gotta be some film buffs here."

Jenny shaded her eyes, scanned the audience, and pointed to the heckler. "No, put your shirt down. I said buffs, not buffed. Nice abs, though. What are you doing later?"

Jenny got a laugh. After doing stand-up for two years, she knew when she won the audience over.

"Yeah, as an actress in musical comedy, I was always cast as the ingénue. Ingénue — that's French for 'prick tease.' The last show I was in was a new musical with a big-time director who shall remain nameless. But you know who you are, you bastard. You're to blame for all of this." She looked up to the heavens and shouted, "You shoulda let me keep the hat!"

Three years earlier, Jenny was living in San Francisco. She just finished her two-mile jog through Golden Gate Park. Like so many women in their early thirties, she was determined to stay in good shape. She paused and took off her San Francisco Giants cap, letting her dark brown hair fall to her shoulders. She crossed the street and headed to her apartment building in the section of the city known as "The Avenues."

Jenny rode the elevator to her third-floor flat, which she shared with her boyfriend Mark, and headed for the shower. Mark, a tall, gangly redhead in his mid-thirties, was engrossed in reading a letter. He sat motionless at the kitchen table, poring over the letter like a cryptographer searching for a clue. He had a tattoo of William Shakespeare on his left bicep that he rubbed as he read, as if trying to summon some alternative meaning from the letter. Jenny came out of the bathroom, toweling off. She displayed her well-maintained figure, but Mark was too morose to notice.

"Hey, Babe, what's in the mail?" she asked.

"Janelle Carter isn't going to do my play."

"What? I thought she accepted it for the next season."

"She did, but her board vetoed it. They won't do two new plays in the same season."

"Gutless," Jenny snarled.

Mark tossed the letter aside. "Screw the Edgeworth Theater and the whole state of Wisconsin."

"You didn't want to go to Wisconsin in January anyway."

He took Jenny's hand and pulled her closer. "I'll put it aside and get back to my bank robber story."

Jenny pulled back and playfully smacked him on the head. "Gotta get dressed. I have an early rehearsal."

"How's it going?" he asked.

"My character Annika is such a cliché. I'm trying to give her some dimension."

Mark grinned as she walked away toweless. "Well, you've got the dimensions, even if she doesn't."

"Save it for tonight."

"Have it your way…and would you mind taking the bus? I need the car to run some errands for the Monarch." Mark Addison was the technical director at San Francisco's Monarch Theater. The City Publicity Office called it a landmark, but those who knew the Monarch called it an old warhorse. Jenny was in rehearsal there for the season's opener, a new musical whose title changed almost daily. Currently, it was Lattes and Lox, with Jenny as the principal character. Mark, thirty-five, and Jenny, three years younger, had been together for two years, but this was the first time they were working on the same show.

The bus dropped Jenny off two blocks from the Monarch. She hustled down the street with her well-used backpack bumping along behind her. But something in a thrift shop window caught her eye, and she stopped for a moment. On display was a hodgepodge of clothing, mismatched china, and a child's dented Radio Flyer wagon. In the wagon was a styrofoam head wearing a knitted wool Sherpa hat with large balls made from yarn dangling down on each side. Jenny went in and emerged a moment later wearing the hat. She looked at her reflection in the window, nodded wickedly, and stuffed the hat into her backpack.

She jogged the last block to the Monarch and passed under the marquee that read, "Coming September 15, Lattes and Lox, with Jenny Corraggio and Ducky Dewson."

An elderly man wearing an usher's cap saw Jennie coming and opened the door for her. "Hey Jenny, you're early!" he yelled as she hurried past him.

"Yeah, call the Guinness Book of Records."

Jenny entered the cavernous Monarch and walked nonchalantly down the aisle. Tommy Milton, the director of the show, sat in the third row, center. He was a man in his sixties, flamboyant and authoritarian. Next to him sat his assistant, a wizened crone with her clipboard at the ready.

Tommy turned to Jenny in mock surprise. "My god, Jenny, is that you? Five minutes early?"

"No, it's my evil twin. The real Jenny will be here in twenty minutes."

Jenny hopped up the steps to the stage, and Tommy hollered after her, "Let me start my heart again."

"Let us know if you find it," she yelled back and disappeared backstage.

The stage was set for the opening scene. It was meant to depict a living room, but the show was behind schedule, and the set was only partially completed. Mark walked back and forth, looking up to check the lights. He called for an assistant on the catwalk above to make some adjustments. Norma, the actress who played Gwen, Jenny's confidante, took her seat in an overstuffed chair. An accompanist sat at a battered upright piano at a far corner of the stage. He vaped and blew clouds of smoke while he chatted with one of the stagehands.

Tommy took the clipboard from The Crone and slammed it on the back of the seat. "All right, all right. Let's get started. We'll begin from Annika's entrance." Tommy turned to talk to his assistant and handed her the clipboard, missing Jenny's entrance. Jenny — as "Annika"— entered wearing her new hat. "Annika" looked dejected, standing on the stage. "Gwen" had the first line.

"OK, Annika, what happened? Did he stand you up?"

Annika barely got the words out, "Worse."

"He made you pick up the check?"

"Even worse. He dumped me."

"Jerry? He dumped you?"

The accompanist set down his vape and, through a cloud of smoke, plunked out the first notes of Annika's song. "He dumped me," Annika sang. "After months and months, he dumped me. I never saw it coming, I thought it couldn't happen to meeeeee. I wore my brand-new sneakers, my hair was in a bun…"

Finally paying attention to the scene, Tommy barked, "OK, stop. Let's stop there." Jenny cracked a wry smile. "What's wrong, Tommy? I'm singing the rewrite, right?"

"Yeah, that's the right version, but you have to lose the hat, sweetheart."

"Lose the hat?" Jenny acted confused. "But the hat is part of Annika's character."

"My love," Tommy explained, "The hat is a distraction from the lyrics — especially the balls."

"But I can't lose the balls," she pleaded. "They're the whole point of the hat. From the very beginning, we discussed that Annika is really nerdy, but unaware of her nerdiness. I'm adding the hat to make that clear. Only Annika would think there's nothing wrong with the hat."

"No, darling. The hat has to go."

"But the costumer thinks it's a great idea."

"Oh, pardon me. The costumer likes it. Well, maybe Ms. Bartholomew would like to take over directing the show, and I'll just sit in the back eating humble pie."

Jenny caved and took off the hat. Mark walked in from the wings and retrieved it from her. Tommy directed "Annika" to take it from the second verse, which she sang with a note of defiance. Satisfied that had he regained the upper hand, Tommy was effusive with his praise. "Great, Jenny, that was super. Even better without the hat."

Tommy called a ten-minute break, and Jenny ran after Mark. He turned to kiss her, but she pulled back.

"Not now, Big Guy. I'm working."

"When we get home, then. We could use a little rehab."

"Right. But where did you put the hat?"

Mark grabbed her shoulder. "Jen, let it go."

"I bought it, and I want it back."

"Oh, all right. I put it in a costume trunk up in the loft. But you can't get up there yet. The paint's still wet."

Jenny rushed past him and into the depths of the Monarch Theater's backstage. The stairway to the loft was freshly painted. A rope hung between the handrails with a "Wet Paint" sign dangling from it. Jenny ran around to the far side of the loft and saw an aluminum extension ladder leading to the second level. She realized the ladder was the way Mark got up to the loft, and she began climbing.

Jenny almost reached the railing of the loft when the ladder slipped, and she fell to the floor below. Mark heard the crash and was the first to reach her, crumpled on the floor, with the ladder resting on top of her.

Hours later, Jenny lay in her hospital bed, hooked up to monitors and an IV. An oxygen tube led up to her nostrils, and her left arm was in a cast. Mark sat next to the bed and held her hand. He jumped up when the orthopedist came in.

"How is she, Doc. The tests come back?" he asked.

The doctor checked her notes before giving the official word. "Ms. Corraggio does have a concussion and major contusions to her left side, along with a simple fracture to the left radius, which should heal quickly. That's the good news."

"The good news?"

"Maybe you should sit down."

Mark groped his way back to the chair and slumped over.

"Ms Corraggio sustained a complete fracture of the T-12 thoracic vertebrae. It's doubtful she'll be able to walk again. However, she'll be given a full course of physical therapy to make sure her upper body remains at full strength."

"Does she know yet?"

"We thought it best to wait until she was completely lucid and you were here, too," she said.

The next morning, Jenny was sitting up in bed when she heard her prognosis. Her first reaction was incredulity. "This is crazy. I'm gonna be in a wheelchair? I'm an actress…and a dancer. I used to be a cheerleader, for chrissake…I can still do cartwheels." She grabbed the monitor cord attached to her chest. "Here, unplug me, and I'll show you."

Mark leaned over and pulled her hand away.

"Mark, you know I'm all right. Tell them I'm all right."

He leaned across the bed and hugged Jenny as she sobbed uncontrollably.

The doctor moved closer and stroked Jenny's hair. "I'm so sorry, Jenny. This is the time when medicine sucks. Absolutely sucks."

Two weeks later, Jenny was sent to physical therapy. During one session, Mark walked in with a bouquet of flowers and watched as Marie, the therapist, knelt in front of Jenny and bent each leg at the knee, held it outstretched for a moment, and replaced the foot on the footplate of the wheelchair.

Mark handed her the flowers and gave her a kiss. "I was going to bring you a Rolex, but you'll have to settle for snapdragons."

Her response was emotionless. "Thanks, sweetie, these will do just fine."

When Marie offered to leave them alone for a bit, Jenny asked her to stay. "I want him to see what we've accomplished."

The therapist resumed the exercise, and Jenny moved on to sarcasm." See, she lifts my legs, and nothing is working. We've been at this for three weeks, and I still don't feel a thing."

"It takes time," Marie explained. "But we don't want you to lose your muscle tone."

"These muscles are tone-deaf," Jenny retorted. "You're wasting your time — and mine." Marie backed away as Mark tried to intervene. Tears flooded from Jenny's eyes.

"I'm sorry, Marie, really, I am. It's just that—"

Mark grasped for something to say, but what came out was weak, and he knew it. "Jenny, don't worry. We'll figure something out." Jenny brushed away her tears and snuffled. "OK, let's look on the bright side. There still are things I can do."

She held the bouquet high above her head with her good arm. "Look, I can play the Statue of Liberty. 'Give me your tired, your poor...' and once this cast comes off, I will raise both hands to heaven that I can still feel my ass on this cushion. Mark, Marie, applause, please." Mark applauded slowly and nodded to Marie, who followed suit.

While Jenny remained in the hospital, Mark spent his days at the Monarch working on another show. Lattes and Lox had moved previews to Minneapolis with a new Annika. The producers decided to open "L&L" away from San Francisco, citing "bad karma" over Jenny's accident. When Mark was not at the hospital, he spent his nights hunched over his laptop, outlining a new play based on a story he heard from a former college roommate about a bank robber on the family tree.

Mark was a recovering alcoholic with three years of sobriety. But his worries over Jenny, along with his concern about job security in the fickle world of theatre, plus growing self-doubt about what he called his "creative mojo," made those nights with his laptop a gamut of distractions.

After his tenth lap around the kitchen and living room failed to shake his gloom, he grabbed his phone and punched in a number he had on speed dial.

"Hello, Bonnie, this is Mark. Are you busy? Look, I need you…No, she's still in the hospital. Won't be back for another week. But right now, I have that feeling, and I need you…I can't leave the apartment, or I'll head straight for the corner liquor store…You have to talk me down…OK, let's chant together…just don't leave me."

Mark sat on the sofa, out of sight of the table and laptop, with his phone to his ear and his head between his knees. He began chanting, "I am strong…I have been strong…I will be strong…I am loved…I have been loved…I will give love…"

After a pot of coffee, Mark reached equilibrium, and the next morning began work on a ramp so Jenny could wheel up to the back door of the apartment and avoid the three steps it took to get there. He checked with the landlord before he began the project, assuring Mr. Chen that everything would be up to code. Mr. Chen was happy to oblige, largely because Mark would be paying for the materials.

Mark heard from a ground-floor tenant that a building inspector had already threatened to fine Chen for not having handicap access to the building. When the inspector returned the next day, the tenant saw Mr. Chen hand him an envelope, and the matter was settled. Mr. Chen's only request was for Mark to paint the plywood and two-by-four ramp silver to make it look like metal. Mark chuckled to himself as he realized creating illusions was not confined to the theatre.

Jenny was in the wheelchair Mark bought at a second-hand store, dressed and ready to go, when Mark rushed into her hospital room. "Sorry. Traffic. You ready?"

"I am so ready to go. Grab my bags and let's get out of here," she said.

Mark grabbed her suitcase and a yellow plastic bag that were lying on the bed. He held the bag toward her. "What's this?"

"Hospital going-away stuff —papers I need to sign, tooth-brush, toothpaste, and an enema. Probably a ladies' urinal, too."

"Sweet," he said.

"Yeah," Jenny said, "just like the swag bags at the Oscars."

Accompanied by Marie, the physical therapist, Jenny wheeled herself down a long hall to an office next to the entrance. While Jenny signed the papers, Mark played solitaire on his phone. Once free of paperwork, Jenny wheeled outside to their car parked at the curb, followed by Mark and Marie. Mark opened the passenger side door, and Jenny pulled up parallel to the front seat.

"That's right, just like we practiced," Marie said.

Mark stood in front of Jenny and crouched down. Jenny threw her arms around his neck, and he began to straighten up. "That's right," Marie said. "Lift with your legs, not with your back, and pivot."

Halfway up, Jenny's arms slipped, and she slid to the curb.

Jenny shrieked, Mark cursed, and Marie stepped in to help steady them. Mark pulled Jenny up, pivoted, and lowered her onto the seat. He bent down and lifted Jenny's legs into the car and shut the door.

"Good job," Marie said. "You did OK. You'll get it." She leaned into the open window and hugged Jenny, just before they drove away.

"Sorry I dropped you," he said.

"No, it was me," she replied. "I let go. I need to strengthen my arms."

Mark parked on the street in front of the apartment and pulled the wheelchair out from behind the driver's seat. This time, the transfer went perfectly. "We're on top of this," Mark said proudly. "We just have to keep it up," Jenny replied.

Mark guided Jenny to the back entrance and mimed a trumpet fanfare. He gave her a pair of scissors and presented the ramp to her, silver, with a red ribbon stretched between the handrails.

She cut the ribbon, but with no enthusiasm, and sat silently at the base of the ramp. Mark asked, "What's wrong, Jen? It'll work. I tested it out with Mr. Chen's wheelbarrow filled with bricks."

"The ramp is fine. It's just that I see my life now, filled with ramps and wheelchairs and people feeling sorry for me." She took a deep breath and wheeled herself up the ramp and down the hall to the elevator.

Mark opened the door to the apartment to reveal books, papers, and a few empty soda cans strewn about the floor and table. When he started to push her over the threshold, she objected.

"Hey, no pushing. The rehab Nazis said I've got to do it all by myself."

"Sorry, I'll try to keep from being helpful."

"The place doesn't look bad. Thanks for cleaning up after all the wild parties."

"No parties, wild or otherwise, I'm afraid."

Jenny wheeled around the room, picking up an empty soda can from the table and tossing it into a wastebasket. Mark hustled to snatch up papers and books from the floor and lay them on the table.

"After I came home from seeing you, I tried to do some writing before I had to get back to work," he explained.

"Lucky you. All I did was play Candy Crush between sessions with the PT. What a freakin' mess. Four weeks in rehab and all I can do is sit in this chair and wheel myself around."

"You learned other things. You did well."

"Stop playing Little Mary Sunshine. All I learned was how to transfer to the toilet and a shower seat."

"And into the car."

"Which I can't drive until we get hand controls. And then where would I go? Back to the theatre? Sure, if they ever do Suddenly, Last Summer, I could play the old bitch in the wheelchair."

"OK, I understand."

"You don't understand. This is Jenny Corraggio for the rest of my life." She turned away from him and paused to regain her composure. "I'm sorry, Mark. I'm so sorry."

"It's OK to vent," he said, and put his arms around her. "Get it all out. But, you've got to stop before you make yourself even more miserable."

"I'll figure something out. I will. I promise."

"I know you will. We will," Mark whispered. Mark's cell phone buzzed, and he fumbled to get it out of his pocket. "Yeah, we're here. Third floor. Apartment 308. Elevator's slow, but it'll get you here."

Mark turned to Jenny, and suddenly his mouth turned dry. "You're about to have a visitor," he said, sheepishly.

"Who?" she asked, as if expecting a negative test result from the hospital.

"Gina's coming to see you. She just got out of a cab."

"Gina? Your Gina?"

"She's not my Gina. She hasn't been for years. You know that," he said.

"Gina McDonald? Over here?"

"She called my cell, actually, she called your cell while you were being checked out," he explained. "She's only in the city for the weekend, and she wanted to see you before she goes back to Chicago."

Jenny leaned forward and nearly fell out of her chair. "You know she's coming to see you. Coming to size up the situation. The vulture hovering over the not-quite-dead-yet carcass. 'Oh, Mark, I'm so sorry your Jenny is a hopeless cripple now. But, as you can see, I'm just fine.'"

"Stop it, Jen. She called and thought you would still be in the hospital. She was sorry she missed you there, so she wants to come to see you here. She caught me off guard, and I told her to come over. Anyway, she's leaving town tonight," he added. "And she's got a boyfriend."

"She always does."

The sound of the doorbell ended their argument abruptly. Jenny sat up and straightened her hair. "Oh, right on cue." Mark approached the door like a man headed in for a colonoscopy. Gina was a tall, very attractive blonde about the same age as Mark. She held a bouquet of flowers. She gave Mark a peck on the cheek and rushed over to Jenny.

"There's our girl." She handed Jenny the bouquet and hugged her. "I don't know what to say, except I'm so glad to see you."

"Well, here I am. Halfway up and about," Jenny responded tonelessly.

"That's what I've been telling her," Mark said.

"Yes, that's what he's been telling me," Jenny sighed.

"Jenny, I can't pretend to understand, but please let me ask if there is anything…Anything I can do for you? I mean, yes, it would be long-distance. My flight leaves at three, but I can call you from Chicago, or text you, from time to time, just to say hello, so you don't feel…so you won't —"

"So I won't feel left out, abandoned, totally out of the scene? Please, keep me posted on what you're doing. I won't be doing anything, but I can fill you in on Mark. He's done lights for all the big shows, including the last one I was in. Or ever will be in. And he's written a play."

"Writing a play," Mark quickly interjected. "It's not finished yet."

"That's wonderful, Mark. What's it about?"

"A girl growing up in Nebraska discovers her grandfather was a bank robber. It's based on a true story, and I'm waiting now for more source material."

"Sounds fascinating. Please send it to me when it's done. I'd love to read it.

"Yes, Mark would like a good courtesy read. Maybe you two could collaborate."

Mark gestured for Jenny to stop her sarcasm with a "cut it out" motion across his neck. "Just sayin'," Jenny said innocently.

"It's OK, Mark. This wasn't the right time for me to come. Jenny, I can only wish you all the best."

Once Gina left, Jenny chucked the bouquet over her shoulder. "I'm sorry," Mark said. "I should have said we weren't ready to have visitors on the first day home."

"Yes, I was a bitch, wasn't I? Why don't you invite some more people over, so we can continue this snarkfest? We're just getting started."

"There's no we in this game. I resign. But I will take the blame for not telling Gina 'no' about coming over here."

"You're such a wuss," she said, as tears welled up in her eyes. "No, I'm sorry, I didn't mean that."

"You sorry you asked me to move in?"

"No. No, it's just that I can't face the idea of being stuck in this apartment for who-knows-how-long."

"Mark dragged over a kitchen chair and sat next to her. "Don't worry, we'll get you out."

Jenny pictured what such an excursion might look like, which made her chuckle. "What, to wheel me around the park for a while and end up at Starbucks for a double mocha?"

"With extra whipped cream," Mark added.

"So I can gain fifty pounds and be a blob on wheels? Fuck that."

"I was thinking more along the lines of taking you to auditions."

"Oh, stop. Just stop," she shouted.

"No, I'm serious," Mark continued. "They're having auditions next week at the Filbert and at the New Avon. I'll take you to both of them. Best thing for you is to get back on the bike...so to speak."

"No friggin' way."

"Jen, this is for me, too. You can start over again and climb up--"

"And climb up the ladder. You were going to say, 'climb up the ladder.'"

"No, I wasn't."

"Yes, you were. ...'Climb up the ladder, climb up the ladder.'"

"That's not what I...Goddamn it!"

"Yes, it was! Yes, it was!" she chanted, as they both started laughing. "Was, too. "Up the ladder, up the ladder...""

Mark choked back his laughter and grabbed Jenny in a hug. "And all fall down," he whispered.

True to his word, and before Jenny might change her mind, Mark drove her to the Filbert Theater the following week. He stood in the back of the house like a nervous parent hoping his kid would make the team. With a script to Who's Afraid of Virginia Woolf in her lap, Jenny glided into a spotlit area center stage. The director and several others were scattered through the front rows.

"You're Jenny Corraggio?" the director asked.

"Yes, I left my resume and headshot at the desk."

"Yeah, I have it here. But it doesn't say anything about…"

"My being in a wheelchair?" Jenny cut in. "I didn't think it would make any difference. I want to try out for the part of Honey. I'm probably too young for Martha."

"You know," he continued, "there's a part in our production of Virginia Woolf where Honey has to dance. Are you able to get up…and dance?"

"Well, I'll admit that I can't get up, but I can dance up a storm on my wheels."

She moved smoothly from side to side and performed a tight pirouette.

"Unfortunately, I don't have any music," she explained, but I had 'In the Mood' in my head. I think George and Martha would play 'In the Mood'."

"Quite possibly. Yes. But let's hear you read a few lines. Honey's monologue on page fifty-three. Honey is unsure of herself, naïve, childlike, a little dim."

"Got it," Jenny said. She took a breath and plunged into Honey's long speech, ending with:

"We took our iced teas and sat under a tree, and I thought he was handsome and charming, and we fell in love right then, or at least I did."

Jenny closed the script and flashed her best ingénue smile at the director.

"That's very nice, Ms. Corraggio. I actually liked it. We'll let you know."

Jenny wheeled up to Mark, still standing at the back of the auditorium.

"You did that well," he said.

"Thanks, but 'we'll let you know' is the old kiss-off. Let's move on."

Next stop, casting for Hamlet at the Avon Theatre. Mark took up his position at the back of the auditorium, and Jenny wheeled onstage.

The director seemed surprised to see her. "Jenny Corraggio. And you're here for …?"

"I'd like to read for a part," Jenny said brightly.

"You realize we're doing Shakespeare, don't you? And this will be staged in authentic Elizabethan dress."

"If the gown is full enough, I can make it work. I've had a lot of practice. I have a big poncho, and I don't have any trouble getting around in the rain."

"I don't think there were any wheelchairs in Hamlet, but we'll have our dramaturg check it out, and we'll be happy to get back to you."

Jenny turned to ice. "This theater is ADA compliant, isn't it? I got in here, didn't I? I got out on the stage, so I should have the chance to act on this stage."

The director asked Jenny to wait a moment. He conferred with the woman sitting next to him. All Jenny could hear was, "… better let her read," and "Oh, very well."

The director put on a big smile. "So, Ms. Corraggio, what would you like to read for?"

"Either Ophelia or Hamlet's mother. May I read for both?"

"How about reading Ophelia. Page sixty-one. Here's the cue — All but one shall live; the rest shall keep as they are. To a nunnery, go."

Jenny glanced at the script and spoke Ophelia's lines from memory, ending with a heartfelt, "O woe is me, to have seen what I have seen, see what I see!"

"Thank you," said the director, without looking up from his notes. "That was very nice. We'll let you know." Jenny countered his cliché. "You'll keep me in mind, right?" And she wheeled out to meet Mark in the lobby.

A few days later, Mark was in a coffee shop near the Monarch Theater waiting to meet Charlie Greenour, one of his old college roommates. Mark nursed his coffee and checked the time on his phone. He hoped Charlie wasn't lost. After the fifth or sixth time-check, Charlie burst through the door like the linebacker he once was. They greeted each other warmly, and Charlie plopped a large Manila envelope on the table.

"Sorry, I'm late. It took me a while to get an Uber to drop Gretchen off at Union Square, then bring me over here."

"How's Gretchen these days?"

"Fine. Just fine. Still spending my money. My only rule for her shopping is that they ship the stuff back home. I'm not carrying it on the plane."

"Good idea," Mark chuckled.

Charlie pushed the envelope over to Mark. "Here's what you wanted, all three of my grandmother's diaries."

"Thanks, man, I really appreciate this," Mark said.

"Photocopies," Charlie whispered. "I keep the originals in my safe at the office. Ray Haskill was my mother's grandfather — the bank robber, a regular Jesse James of the 1930s. And you know what? Nobody ever guessed it was him. It was my grandmother's legwork that found it all out."

"It's a story that's worth telling. Hell, Charlie, you should be writing it."

"You're the writer. I just run a car dealership," Charlie said.

"This story will make a helluva play. God, what your grandmother must have gone through. I've already got it outlined, and this will put the meat on the bones. Charlie, I really do appreciate this.

Charlie waved him away. "It's all yours. I owe you. The night you pulled me out of that bar, I know I would have killed the guy. I still have flashbacks about it."

"We were all very drunk. Anderson, too. Amazing the cops never came after us."

"I've tapered off. Kids'll do that for you. How 'bout you, Mark? Still tippin' more than a few?"

Mark sat back in his chair. "It's been a struggle. Going on three years sober, but it's still one day at a time. A.A. didn't work for me. Once I got my three-month chip, I'd fall back off the wagon. Never could get past three months. No, the only thing that works for me is one-on-one therapy. I see a therapist once a week. That, and I'm in a relationship with a fantastic woman."

"The actress who had the accident?"

"How did you know?"

"Gina told Gretchen," Charlie said. "They still stay in touch with each other on Facebook."

Mark crumpled his empty coffee cup. "Oh, shit, Gina? She just keeps popping up like herpes. All I need is for Jenny to hear Gina's been spreading the news."

Charlie decided to get off the topic of Gina. "You doin' all right? Financially, I mean? Therapy costs money."

"I'm fine. Really, I am. Two years ago, Jenny asked me to move in with her so we could share expenses. I let my landlord buy me out of my rent-controlled apartment, so that's given us a little stash, and I can stay in therapy. But it's really Jenny who keeps me out of trouble with the booze."

"She keeps after you, huh?"

"No, it's not like that. She has an effect on me. A good effect. I just can't let her down. It was that way before. And now, more than ever."

Charlie punched him on the shoulder. "Sounds like love to me."

"It's more complicated than that."

"Friends with benefits?"

Mark tried to hold back a smile. "Yeah, I guess so. Lots and lots of benefits." Mark stood up to avoid any more questions from his friend. "You have time for a tour of my place of employment?" he asked.

"Sure, I'm a free man until Gretchen calls to have me come get her. She wants to go to Fisherman's Wharf again." Mark grabbed the envelope and they walked out, stepping over a man passed out in the entranceway.

The next day, Jenny got a visit from an old friend. Jenny was furiously pulling a rubber stretch band across her chest, letting it snap, and then pulling again. A knock at the door cut her exercise session short. Norma appeared in the doorway.

"Norma! Oh, my god. Get in here."

Norma paused to size Jenny up before running over to give her a long embrace.

"It's so good to see you," Jenny whispered through her sobs.

"I just got back into town and dropped my bags at my apartment. Geez, my place stinks. I don't think my house sitter ever cleaned the litter box. But I had to come right over. How are you? How are you doing?"

Jenny spun around to show off her new wheelchair, a sportier version, like the wheelchairs basketball players use, courtesy of Mark's friend Charlie.

"How do you like my new wheels? I just got 'em."

"Great. They look great on you. What's up with you now?"

"Taking my pills, doing my exercises, reading scripts. I've started going to auditions."

"Good for you. When do you get out of the chair?"

Jenny looked away from her friend. "Not for a while. Probably never."

"No, no. Jenny, you're not serious, are you?"

"Afraid so. This is Jennifer Marie Corraggio from now on." She tried to put on a brave face, but Norma could see right through it. "That's OK," she continued. "I still have my dreams, without an agent, of course. Freddy said he couldn't find me anything, and finally, he stopped calling altogether. I'm going to auditions on my own."

"Good for you. You have your dreams — and they'll be fulfilled, I believe it. You're strong. I mean strong-willed…and… and…I'm sorry, I'm babbling here. It's just that this news —"

"Yeah, it hit me pretty much the same when I heard it."

Norma groped for the chair behind her. "I think I need to sit down."

"Enough of this gloom," Jenny said. "How did the show go in Minneapolis?"

"Well…It was…"

"Tell me, I want to know."

"Sorry, I didn't think you'd want to hear about it. Bad memories for you."

"It's OK. I confess, I haven't followed it. I didn't want to be reminded. But I'm OK with it now, and I want to hear how you did with it. You were sweet to not text me about the show, just the Minnesota weather, and trying lutefisk…So?"

"It bombed. It was a mess. Rewrites every day. They even changed the title. It's now Love, Loss, and Licorice."

Jenny let out a roar of laughter that left her breathless. "I don't believe it," she gasped.

"Yep, and it closed after a week. The new Annika was shaky. She could sing, but she was as stiff as a three-day-old corpse. The show needed you, Jenny. Fourteen people stuck in East Jesus, Minnesota. Word is, some of them never got paid."

"I'm sorry. I never thought —"

"Shit happens. It's a fragile business for everyone. It gets tough if we all don't pull together."

"Ouch," Jenny said.

"I didn't mean — sorry I said anything. Forget it. You took it the toughest."

Jenny looked down and played with the exercise band. "I won't forget. I can't. I'm really sorry. All this time, I thought you were touring the Midwest with the show."

"Oh, I toured, all right. I was lucky to land on my feet — sorry, bad choice of words. I was Aunt Eller in Oklahoma. I replaced an aging actress in Storm Lake, Iowa. She broke her hip in the middle of the hoedown, and Billy Weaver called me. Honestly, I was checking the Greyhound schedule to come back here — OK, enough of my troubles, how are you and Mark doing?"

"Mark has been an angel. He visited me every day in the hospital."

"I always liked Mark. You should have asked him to move in a long time ago."

"It's been two years, but I'm worried now. I have to show him I can get along on my own — which I can. I was afraid he'll start seeing me only as an invalid, someone he has to be responsible for. And then he'll get tired of the whole situation — of me."

"You know he wouldn't do that," Norma scolded.

"I hope not. But the fear is still there, hovering in the background." Jenny squeezed the band more tightly. "Anyway, we made a pact — he can leave any time, and I can kick him out anytime."

"How romantic," Norma said archly. "But I know you guys can make it work. You've got a good thing going. Not like me and Alfred. Good riddance to that self-centered putz."

Mark pushed the door open, carrying a toolkit. "Hey, Norma, were you talking about me?"

He set the bag on the kitchen table and hugged Norma. "So, how long you been back?"

"About an hour ago. Jenny can fill you in. I've got to skedaddle."

"Hey, don't let me run you off," Mark said.

"No, I've got a litter box I've gotta face up to. Jenny can explain. I'll call you tomorrow."

"Thanks, Norma. I'll talk to you," Jenny yelled.

Jenny turned to Mark and said, with finality, "She hates me."

Mark was dumbfounded and tried to process her remark. "What are you saying?"

"Norma's mad at me because the Annika show closed in previews, and the cast was left in the lurch. Without paychecks. She said if I were still in it, it might have worked."

"What? Norma? That's crazy. That show would have bombed no matter who was in it."

"Yeah, but still —"

"But still? Look what happened to you. It's not like you walked out on it."

"Very funny."

"Come on, Jen. You know what I mean. Hey, you're still auditioning. Have you heard anything?"

"Yeah. I got it, and they shot it today. I took the bus over, but that's another story," Jenny sighed.

"Hey, that's fantastic! You did it, I knew you would! Time for champagne — for you."

"It's a Toyota commercial."

"That's great, Jen. You're off and…wheeling."

"You got that right. And at about five seconds from the end, the music rises, the balloons fall, and customers rush to the cars. Then, I wheel across the screen, and the camera zooms in on a little boy holding a puppy. I saw the final take."

"OK, it's not Medea."

"Don't you see? I open for a fucking puppy. How pathetic is that?"

"Well, it's not your best work, but —"

"Why don't you wheel me out into the hall and push me down the stairs? Put me out of my misery. I lost everything, including my dignity. Don't you understand? I wish you could spend a day — no, just an hour in this chair and see how you feel."

"I know what you're thinking," he said, and then plunged into a Brooklyn accent. "You coulda been a contendah. And you still can be…with your talent…and drive."

Jenny wheeled so close to him that she rammed his shins with her footplates. "You're not listening to me. I hate this. I just hate it."

He bent down to hug her, but she backed up and started to sob. "Mark, I don't want to give it up. Help me not give it up."

"Jen, you're going to make it. You're too strong not to. Listen to me, please. I've had an idea running through my head, and I guess now is the time to spill it."

Mark backed away and began a formal pitch like he would to a producer.

"I think you're perfect to do —and no pun intended here — you're perfect to do…stand-up."

Jenny stared silently at him before responding with measured calm.

"Stand-up. Stand-up, as in stand-up comedy? Is this a line from one of your stories?"

"No, I'm dead serious. You're perfect for stand-up. You're a great comic actor. Your timing's impeccable. You have an edge to you. You've got all the tools —"

"Yeah, including a wheelchair."

"See! See! Edgy. Quick and edgy. And we can work out the material. But you've got a story that makes you unique."

"Oh, I'm unique, all right. You want me to come off as an edgy, surly cripple? Thanks for the thought, but you're nuts."

"Jenny, you can do this. You're funny; you're quick. It's worth a shot."

She continued her silent stare.

"Or you can keep on opening for fucking puppies."

A month later, Jenny and Mark found themselves backstage at Shady Lady, a topless, pole-dance bar in Modesto, California, about a two-hour drive east of San Francisco. Mark landed Jenny's first gig through a fellow electrician who did side jobs to supplement her theater income. Mark and Jenny came up with twenty minutes' worth of material, which Jenny tried out in front of Norma and two students from clown college. They laughed, they applauded, and they were too kind.

Raunchy music drifted backstage at Shady Lady's as Mark watched Jenny wheel back from the stage. She looked exasperated.

"Thank you, Modesto, thank you. And the horse you rode in on," she grumbled to no one in particular.

"It's a start," Mark said, grasping for a kernel of positivity. "Look at it this way, Modesto is where George Lucas grew up."

"Yeah, but he left, ya know. I don't know what's worse — opening for a puppy or being sandwiched between tits and asses. You think I could learn to pole dance in my wheelchair?

"Not without chafing," he replied.

Offstage, a woman began shouting. It was Glenda, one of the pole dancers, yelling at a drunken patron.

"Keep your hands off, you sunnavabitch. All you paid for was beer."

Glenda, wet-hen furious, walked backwards from the wings. She was wearing a short kimono, ballet slippers, glittery thong, and a tiara. She carried a glittery "magic wand" with a star at one end. It was apparent she was wearing nothing but the thong under the kimono, which she held together in her off hand. Still facing offstage, she flipped the bird to someone out in the wings. When she turned around, Jenny and Mark's presence gave her a jolt.

"Oh. Hi, guys. Don't worry, it's just another night at the O.K. Corral." She waved the wand toward them. "Hi, I'm Glenda — Glenda the Good Bitch."

She waved the wand toward them again. "Get it?"

"Yeah, we get it," Jenny said. "Sorry, we didn't mean to scare you."

"I'm Mark, and this is Jenny."

"My pleasure, Glenda said. "I'd shake your hand, but if I let go of this robe, we'll all be embarrassed. Hey, hon, hold my wand while I tie up."

"Just so you don't try to hold his wand," Jenny responded dryly.

Glenda handed Mark the wand and tied her kimono.

"I liked your act, even if those bozos didn't. You've got guts. Is that wheelchair a gimmick?"

"No, it's real. I had an accident, and this is me from now on."

"An accident! Me, too. Car crash?" Glenda asked and looked concerned.

"No, I fell off a ladder."

"Mine was a motorcycle. I was on the back, and we whipped around a corner, and I got thrown against a parked car. Broke my shoulder and both ankles. That was the end of my career. I was in a ballet company up in Oregon, the Portland Ballet."

"Yeah, Portland Ballet," Mark piped up. "I did a lighting gig there a couple of years ago."

"You're the first person in this town who's heard of it," Glenda said. "Even after rehab, I couldn't continue. Funky ankles, and I gained a little weight and got top-heavy, which helps in this business, if you know what I mean. So, I moved back down here. My real name is Edie Wexler. Single mom supporting my daughter.

She's three. She thinks I'm a singer in a fancy restaurant; only my sister knows. She bought me a gun, which I won't use. Just to satisfy her, I keep it in the car between the front seats in a tampon box."

Mikey, the club owner, emerged from her office. She was a woman with a buzz cut and a face like a bulldog. "OK, Glenda, you're up again," she barked.

"You get rid of that creep?" Glenda asked.

Mikey snorted. "Yeah, the cops were sitting in the parking lot, and they took him away. If you want to press charges, you'll have to go down to the courthouse in the morning."

"Who has the time for that? He'll catch holy hell when his wife has to pick him up from jail." She waved her wand at Jenny and Mark. "Nice talking to you. Thanks for letting me blab. Good luck to you, sweetie."

Glenda pliéd before pirouetting onstage. When she let her kimono slip to the floor, she was wearing nothing but her tiara, thong, and ballet slippers. And she carried the wand.

Mikey walked over to Jenny with an envelope. "OK, hon, I gave you a shot. But let me give you a piece of advice. If you want to make it in this business, you'd better dirty up your act, know what I mean? Guys out there ain't comin' for Sunday School."

Mark thanked her for what would be good advice.

Mikey started to hand Jenny the envelope.

"What's this?"

"Your split of tonight's tips. Nine dollars."

As Jenny reached for the envelope, she doubled over, with her head between her knees.

"Mark, help me up, please."

Mark rushed over and sat her up.

"Is she alright?" Mikey asked.

"Yeah, just a spasm," Mark said, swallowing his concern. "It happens every once in a while."

Jenny took the envelope and tried to fluff off the incident. "No worries. Weak back, strong mind is all."

Mikey observed them for a moment, wished them well, and went back to her office.

"Maybe I should be doing this topless," Jenny said. "Give me another dollar, and we can get two small lattes at Peet's."

"What do you think?" he asked. "Are you still up for this?"

"Damn straight. Where to next?"

"Next weekend, a real comedy club in Fresno," he announced with comically overblown pride.

Jenny matched his enthusiasm. "Fresno, the gateway to Bakersfield!"

They laughed and high-fived before Jenny turned serious. "That old gal was right. We gotta get edgier."

"You talkin' about blue humor?" he asked.

Jenny winked. "Well, powder blue, at least."

Their mini-comedy tour took them south from Shady Lady's to Fresno, Bakersfield, and finally, to Oxnard. To stretch their funds, they slept in the car. Along the way, Jenny honed her act to where she drew more laughs than groans. But both of them knew she had a long journey ahead. After the gig, they parked in the far corner of the strip-mall lot where the Laff Riot was squeezed between a Taekwondo studio and a pet grooming store. Mark and Jenny reclined in the seats and stretched out.

"Do you think we stink?" Mark asked.

"Not at all," Jenny answered. "They loved me here in Oxnard. Whodathunkit? Oxnard!"

"No, I mean here in the car. We've been sleeping here for what...two weeks?"

"Geez, do I have a crick in my neck?" she said.

"Me too. But if the take is good in Irvine, we can get a motel room."

"Good, then you can check my butt for pressure sores."

"I'll be ready."

"You're my absolute hero," she said and leaned over and kissed him. "You know what I hate most about all this? Gas station restrooms. This one was OK, but that last one was nasty."

"For me, it's Egg McMuffins," he declared.

"I thought you liked Egg McMuffins."

"I did, but this trip I'm McMuffin-ed out.

Suddenly, a woman knocked on the driver's side window. It was Sylvia Mandelbaum, a woman in her sixties, fast talking, well dressed, and self-assured. She wore large dangling earrings and rows of clattering bracelets on each wrist.

Mark sprang to attention. "It's all right, Officer. We're about to get back on the road."

"I'm not a cop. Roll down your window," Sylvia shouted, and Mark complied.

"I caught your act tonight, and I've been looking for you since you left. They said you were out here, and — can I get in the back? I'm freezing my ass out here."

Mark and Jenny looked at each other and shrugged, as if to say, "OK, I guess."

"You'll have to go around the other side. Her wheelchair is over here," Mark told her. "My first groupie." Jenny giggled and rubbed her hands together. "This is exciting."

With a clattering of bracelets, Sylvia climbed into the back seat. "I was visiting my son here in Oxnard, and he took me to this club. I liked your act. I'm from L.A. I'm an agent, and I want to work with you."

She reached out and shook Jenny's hand, ignoring Mark.

"I'm Sylvia Mandelbaum — maybe you've heard of me."

"Well, we have now," he said.

"Jenny Corraggio — real name or stage name?" Sylvia asked.

"It's my real name."

"Good. Ethnic and memorable. This wheelchair — real or a prop?"

"It's real, I'm afraid. I can't walk."

"Good. Authenticity is good. SAG? AFTRA? Equity?"

"All of them."

"Good. That puts us at scale, at least."

She turned to Mark. "I didn't get your name. You her manager?"

"Mark Addison. I'm her —"

"He's my lover," Jenny cut in.

"Oooh, good. Good angle. Good for People magazine and the afternoon talks. Look, I know you don't have an agent. An agent would have you announce where you're playing next. From now on, that's what you do. Where's your next gig?"

"Irvine…the Comedy Castle. She's there for a week. I booked her through a college buddy."

"Good for you." Sylvia acted unimpressed with Mark's connection. "Irvine, eh? Orange County. I got some lines to add to your show for that crowd. Gotta cause a stir."

"I think we're pretty stirring right now," Jenny said.

"You are, sweetheart, but you have to branch out. Never leave a stone unturned, as I always say. I can get you a booking at the Comedy Workshop in West L.A. in two weeks. Here's my card."

Sylvia handed each of them a card. "I'll catch up with you in Irvine."

Knowing how to make a memorable exit, she pulled herself out of the car but held on to the door. "And don't worry, it's the standard fifteen percent." She slammed the door and disappeared into the darkness of the parking lot.

"I don't believe this," Jenny exclaimed. "The Comedy Workshop! Annika is avenged!" Mark watched her get something from her coat pocket. It was Annika's crazy hat. She pulled it down over her ears. "I've been carrying it for luck, and now it's time to bring it out again."

Mark was dumbfounded. "How'd you get that?"

"The costumer had it. She mailed it to me."

Mark shook his head. "I have to admit, the hat was a good idea."

"Thanks, sweetie," she said, and with tears streaming down her face, she hugged him with all the strength she could muster.

She wiped away her tears and whispered, "You know, my Visa isn't quite maxed out. Let's go get a motel room. It'll be great to get horizontal for a change."

Mark grinned. "Good idea. I'll be ready."

"That's my boy," she said.

At the club in Irvine, Jenny "killed it," as they say. So she went into the Comedy Workshop in Los Angeles with renewed confidence. She was in the middle of her monologue when she pulled out the Sherpa hat and put it on. Laughs erupted as she struck various poses wearing the hat, moving from silly to naughty and back again.

"My boyfriend loves this hat," she began. "Go ahead and say it, 'Jenny, it's you.' I like to wear it when he's out of town, just to remind me of him."

The tassels swung back and forth.

"Oh, come on, use your imagination. You know what I'm sayin'. When no one's around, there's always your electric toothbrush. Am I right, ladies?"

She pointed at a man in the audience.

"Hey, Mister, I wasn't talking to the dudes. And in your case, I don't wanna know."

"I don't wanna know, because, basically, I don't wanna make trouble. But trouble happens to me. It's like when I get on the bus. People on the bus get pissed off because they know the driver is gonna have to lower the wheelchair lift, which takes 22 seconds. I've timed it. Then, he's gonna have to ask the person sitting in the fold-up seat to get up, which makes their day, y'know. Then, he has to strap my chair to the floor and buckle me in. And the whole time, I see people rolling their eyes and checking their watches. The tension mounts, so I say, "What's the matter? Can't a girl enjoy a little bondage once in a while?""

"Hey, speaking of bondage, my friend Judy just had a baby."

She pointed at a woman in the audience. "Yeah, you get it, don't you? Babies keep you in bondage until the kid is eighteen."

"Judy's baby is a cute one…I guess. If you don't mind the drool. I think she learned it from the dog, this big old boxer. Drool comin' down both sides. Dog's name is Shasta. They named the baby after the dog. They'll probably have to lock the kid in her room every summer, like my parents did with me.

"But they let me out for my first job, which was at a bar. Some kids at my school had early morning shifts at Wendy's. Before I went to school, I cleaned up at the Tiki-Tiki Club. Had to mop the restrooms and refill the condom machine. Ever see the brands they have in there? Sky Rocket? Partner's Pleasure? Slip 'n' Slide?

My favorite was Tropical Delight. Had a picture of a pineapple on it. Whoa, walk on the wild side. And the graffiti on the walls. Lots of drawings, not to scale, of course. And the phone numbers. 'For a good time, call.' So, one morning, I decided to call one of the numbers." She mimed talking on the phone. "Hi, Aunt Sophie, am I interrupting anything?"

"Hey, you've been a great audience. Thank you, L.A. Thank you all."

Jenny waved and wheeled offstage to a hearty applause.

Six weeks later, Jenny and Mark found themselves in a Los Angeles apartment just off Wilshire Boulevard, near the La Brea Tar Pits. They sold their San Francisco furniture, which included a pair of antique chests Jenny had inherited. They had lived in the L.A. apartment with thrifted leftovers.

Jenny sat at the still-serviceable table, typing on a laptop, with an open can of Diet Coke and a black three-ring binder beside her. Sylvia came in from the hall, juggling a vase of flowers and talking on her cell phone. She kicked the door closed without missing a beat.

"No, that's too far out. She's just interviewed Kitty Carter, and we have to keep the momentum going. No, she kept it clean…Yeah, well…look, you gotta get her a slot on the fourteenth or fifteenth, no later. I've got a tentative on CBS for the same time, but I'm givin' you a break here…NO, I don't bullshit…"

She winked at Jenny. "Call me by end-of-day. Bye."

Sylvia handed Jenny the flowers. "Here, these are for you. They were downstairs."

"Who are they from?" Jenny asked.

"Somebody named Norma. Sounds like she's apologizing for something."

"You read the card?" Jenny asked indignantly.

"Of course, I read the card. I'm your manager. That's what I do."

Jenny relaxed and read the card. "'Congrats on your success in L.A. Sorry I put my foot in my mouth. You're the best. Love, Norma.' That's so sweet, and it means a lot. But who was on the phone?"

"Annie Markus over at Channel Five. I've known her for years. Where's Mark?"

"I sent him to the supermarket. We're out of Diet Coke, cottage cheese, and toilet paper."

"That's a combination.

"Yeah, I'm making a casserole tonight."

"I'll pass on the dinner invitation, then. How's the book coming?"

Under Sylvia's direction, Jenny signed a book contract, a memoir of her two careers so far. Sylvia convinced the publisher that the book would fill "at least half a dozen niches." The contract came with a small advance, which Sylvia negotiated up from zero.

"The writing's slow, I'm afraid. I keep getting these twinges in my tailbone, and it's hard to concentrate."

"At least you can feel down there," Sylvia said.

"Mark tells me it's phantom butt pain."

"What a sweetheart," Sylvia sighed.

"I'm thinking of putting it in the act, but 'phantom butt pain' might be too obscure."

"Not in West Hollywood!" Sylvia cackled.

"Maybe I'll try it out at The Workshop."

"You're still doing the 'Clash of Careers' joke, aren't you?"

"Oh, yeah. It's a killer, but I need to set it up better."

Jenny winced and reached around to rub her back. "Crap, I was trying to hold off, but now I need some pain pills. Syl, open that drawer in the table and get me my Gabapentin."

Sylvia went to the table, opened the drawer, and held up two bottles. "OxyContin…Hydrocodone, that's what you need."

"No, that stuff puts me to sleep. I keep it for when the pain is really bad. Gabapentin targets my tailbone, not my head. It's the yellow ones."

Sylvia rummaged around and found the Gabapentin and took the bottle to Jenny, who dumped two pills into her hand and swallowed them with a swig of Diet Coke.

Sylvia's phone buzzed. "I have to take this. It's my daughter."

"Hi, Deb…Yes, I have thought about it, and I still think it's a bad idea. Can't help you on this one. Why don't you ask your dad? …No, I'm not going to talk to him… You talk to him. Put some pressure on him, and he'll cave. And leave me outta this. Bye."

"Be glad you don't have a kid. She wants twenty thousand to

go into business with a partner. Two years in and out of rehab, and she wants to open a cannabis store."

"She'd probably be good at it. How long's she been clean this time?"

Sylvia threw up her hands. "Who knows? She says a year."

"Mark's going on four. You know, the best bartender I ever met was a recovering alcoholic. Made the best martinis ever. He used sweet pickles instead of olives."

"Sounds disgusting."

"He said it was his signature drink. You hear a lot of crazy stories in bars. When Mark and I were on the road, we played this real dive. Pole dancers, over-priced champagne, V.I.P. Room, the whole thing. We met this dancer who went by Glenda the Good Bitch — tiara, magic wand, and nothing else. For protection, she kept a gun in her car, in a tampon box. A good idea, really. That's where my mother used to keep her stash."

"That's a helluva story, Jen. You should put it in the book."

Jenny patted the black binder next to her laptop. "Glenda's already there. I'm printing it out as I go."

Suddenly, Mark burst through the door with a grocery bag, waving two tabloid newspapers. Whiplash Films was emblazoned on the back of his jacket.

"Did you see this? Did you see this? Front page of The Hollywood Tatler."

He reads, "Photogs catch Jenny Corraggio out of wheelchair walking down Rodeo Drive." What kind of crap is this? Makes

Jenny look like a fraud."

Sylvia grabbed the papers and scrutinized them, then looked up, smiling. "This is great. What a gift."

"Are you nuts?" Mark raged. "This will kill us."

"No, this is pure gold. Jenny's now in every checkout line in L.A."

"Walking down Rodeo Drive. How many people would know this was photoshopped?

"Relax, Mark. No one believes what's in these giveaway rags. And anyone who does believe it wouldn't be in our audience anyway."

"Makes her look like a phony," he retorted.

"But a funny phony. Sylvia's right, it's all about getting my name out there."

"Sylvia's right! Sylvia's always right. She's been right ever since she met us."

"Ahh, Mark, please." Jenny tried to soothe him.

"Don't 'Ahh, Mark' me. I'm not in the mood. Anyway, I have to get to work."

"But it's already five o'clock."

"It's a late call. We're shooting a night scene on top of a parking garage up in the Hollywood Hills. You know, where you can see the L.A. skyline stretched out below. The location has been used a zillion times. Sure, it's a cliché, but not to Whiplash Films L-T-D. They've got twelve naked cheerleaders, a Neanderthal fullback, and I get to light the money shot."

Mark grabbed his toolkit and stormed out, slamming the door behind him.

"I'm sorry, Syl. He's been stressed because of his new job. He's afraid he's in over his head."

"What?!" Sylvia exclaimed. "In this town? Nobody thinks like that. Or if they do, they run back to Kansas or Delaware or someplace. What's he doing this time?"

"He's an associate production manager at Whiplash Films."

"Small potatoes, even for the porn industry."

"Well, Whiplash is film, not theater, and that's what worries him. He doesn't like the job, but at the same time, he's afraid of screwing up."

"Sweetie, nobody here ever screws up. You just blame somebody else. That's what personal assistants are for. Tell Mark to get himself one." She took Jenny's hands in hers. "Look, I know Mark feels like I'm an intruder, but we're doing business here."

"I think he understands that. I'll talk to him when he gets back."

"Good girl. But when you see him, don't tell him I planted that story."

"You what?!"

"I have friends in low places. I know the publisher."

"That's terrible," Jenny giggled and threw a pen at her manager.

"No, that's show business. I have to get home. I'll see you tomorrow."

With Sylvia gone, Jenny turned back to her laptop.

The Whiplash Films shoot in the Hollywood Hills did not go as planned. Six of the actresses were no-shows, and the other six constantly complained about how cold it was, even though they were given robes and Uggs to wear between takes. The cold also had a negative effect on the fullback's performance. In addition to a robe, he was given a pair of handwarmers to tuck into his shorts.

"Dude, this has never happened to me before," he told the director, who was not sympathetic.

After twelve takes and the endless shaking of pom-poms, they called it a wrap in every sense of the word. Mark considered looking for other work.

The next morning, Sylvia came into the apartment, followed by her daughter, Debbie, a woman in her early twenties, carrying Sylvia's briefcase. Sylvia was, as usual, dressed professionally. In contrast, Debbie wore jeans, sneakers, and a jacket over a t-shirt from some band's world tour.

"Ready for your photo shoot?" Sylvia shouted.

Jenny wheeled out of the bedroom, wearing a pink T-shirt under a black leather jacket.

"Hey, you look great," Sylvia said. "Perfect look for a publicity shot for the new show."

"Jenny," she continued, "this is my daughter, Debbie. She's going to be my personal assistant for a while."

"Oh, that's great. It's about time you got one." She reached out to shake Debbie's hand but got a fist-bump instead. "Debbie, welcome aboard…What are your plans for Debbie?"

"I think we'll start by —"

Debbie cut her mother off. "I'm just a gofer. Whatever Mom wants, I guess."

"Oh, come on, you've got to start somewhere in this business. Today a P.A., tomorrow a director."

"I don't want to be in this business. I just need to raise enough money so my partners and I can buy into a cannabis shop."

"It's been her goal for months now," Sylvia said with resignation.

"I want to put away seven grand by the end of the year. My dad says that whatever I have by then, he'll match two for one." She turns to her mother. "Dad's a dick. He couldn't just give me the money, could he?"

"Her father's in public television. He's into matching gifts."

"And he's a dick," Debbie emphasized.

"That's not for you to say," Sylvia said.

Jenny decided to cut the squabble. "Hey, folks, we'd better get moving. My appointment is at eleven o'clock. Sylvia, get me the bottle of baclofen out of the pill drawer. I don't want to start spazzing in the middle of the shoot."

Sylvia went to the little table with a vase of flowers on it. Debbie watched with interest as Sylvia slid open the drawer and took out a small prescription bottle.

"We'll be shooting stills, so I want to be able to sit still."

Jenny stuffed the bottle into her pocket.

The door swung open, and Mark dragged himself in. He dropped his toolbox, causing a loud crash. Jenny gingerly asked how his day went.

"I'm beat. We were there until sun-up. I lost track of the number of takes, but we finally got one. I never thought I'd be sick of being around a bunch of naked women."

"Mark, this is Debbie, Sylvia's daughter. She's going to be Sylvia's P.A."

"That means I'm her gofer."

"Could be worse," Mark said. "You could be a naked cheerleader."

"I'm sorry?" Debbie said, taking offense.

"Never mind. Nice to see you folks, but I'm beat. I'm gonna go crash. Have a nice day, all of you."

Jenny gave Mark a half-hearted wave as he retreated to the bedroom.

Sylvia took command and told them to hustle. "I had to park two blocks away. Get the door, Deb, and I'll push Jen."

Debbie held the door open, and Sylvia pushed Jenny into the hall. But Debbie remained in the doorway and yelled after them, "I have to use the restroom. You two go ahead; I'm parked right behind you. I'll meet you there."

Debbie closed the door quietly and slipped over to the pill drawer. Mark suddenly appeared in the bedroom doorway and watched as Debbie rooted through the drawer until she found the

OxyContin. She dropped the bottle into Sylvia's briefcase.

"Why don't you leave her just one?" he said softly, making Debbie jump in surprise. "I'm a light sleeper. Now, take that bottle out of your briefcase."

Debbie quickly fished out the pills. "I was just curious to see what she was taking. I know about drugs and how bad they can be." It was a lame response, and she knew it.

"I know what's in that drawer. Open the bottle and dump the pills into my hand."

Debbie did as Mark said. He took one pill out of his hand and balled his fist over the rest of them.

"Hold the bottle up," he said, and Debbie complied. Mark dropped the single pill into the bottle, capped it, and dropped the bottle into the drawer.

"We'll leave her the one. She doesn't need to have the rest around now."

Debbie watched Mark pull the flowers out of the vase, drop the handful of pills into the water, and return the flowers to the vase.

"You staying clean? I know it's a struggle."

"Just beer and pot. Nothing stronger. No pills, no needles."

"I have three years of sobriety, and it's still not easy. You have anyone to talk to if you get the itch?"

"I have a sponsor," she said.

"Good, but if you need anyone else, give me a call."

She brushed a tear from her cheek. "Thanks. I will."

"Good. Now, get out of here. Get back to work, and don't do anything stupid."

Early the next morning, Jenny was in her wheelchair, once again doing arm exercises with a stretch band. Mark opened the front door so quietly that Jenny didn't hear him. When she did, she jumped and let out a shriek.

"What are you — Mark, where have you been?"

"Out. Just driving around. Thinking. Slept in the car for a while. I was trying to work things out in my head before I came home."

"So, you're home. So, talk to me."

"Remember our pact?" he asked. "You have the right to kick me out anytime, and I have the right to leave."

"Oh, Mark, I know we haven't had much time for each other these past couple of months —"

"Jenny, you don't need me anymore."

"Mark, that's not—"

"Just listen to me, will you? Hear me out. I feel totally useless around here. You've got your caregiver, your physical therapist, and you've got Sylvia. You haven't bounced an idea off me in ages, like we used to. I'm of no help. I have a job I hate. I mean, I had a job — I quit this morning after the shoot."

"That's great, baby. I know how it makes you feel. Just take some time off, so you can —"

"Don't get me wrong, I'm thrilled — thrilled — with your

success," he said. "I'm not jealous. I want you to have what you've achieved and more. But I need something for me. I need to get away."

"I thought we were a team," she said.

"That was then, and this is now. You're in the Majors, and I'm stuck down in Double-A. You don't need me. Look, this is great for you, and I'm really happy for you. But I need to get out on my own. I'm going to Chicago to work with Michael Kurkowitz on a new concept theatre company he's starting. Michael's a genius, you know that, and he wants to do the play I sent him."

"Bullshit! It's not Michael Kurkowitz, it's me. Me and this fucking wheelchair and my useless legs and my dependency. And for God's sake, don't say, 'It's not you, it's me.' Spare me that, all right?"

"Jen, please don't make this any harder than it is. I just came back to get my stuff."

He walked into the bedroom, returning with a suitcase.

"You already packed?" she asked, her voice breaking. "When?"

"Last week. I was depressed, and I knew I'd have to do this eventually."

He kissed her on the top of her head. "I'm proud of you, and I can only wish the best for you."

Mark quickly turned away from her, and Jenny watched the door close. She felt a twinge as she heard him lock the door behind him.

She sang softly to herself:

"He dumped me.

After months and months,

He dumped me.

I never saw it coming.

I thought it couldn't happen

To me."

Jenny slowly wheeled over to the pill drawer. She pulled it open and rummaged around until she found the right pill bottle. "To sleep, perchance to dream an OxyContin dream," she whispered.

She unscrewed the top and dumped the contents into her hand. Only one pill fell out. She shook the bottle and peered inside as if it were a microscope.

"One! One pill! Where'd they go?" Suddenly realizing who the culprit was, she screamed, "Mark, you bastard!"

After a string of expletives, some of them learned from her Italian grandmother, she threw the pill across the room. Sobbing, Jenny wheeled over to the couch and tried to transfer from her chair. But she missed and slid onto the floor. She attempted to pull herself up to the wheelchair but only managed to push it away. She took a deep breath before trying to maneuver herself up onto the couch, but she couldn't twist herself around to use both arms.

"Dammit, where's my phone?"

She groped around as far as she could reach, but still couldn't find her cell phone until she realized it was still on the table.

She looked around the room to survey her predicament, and then sobbed, "Help, I've fallen, and I can't fucking get up." Exhausted, she yanked a pillow off the couch. Too worn out to cry anymore, she lay her head down on it and curled up in a fetal position.

Later that morning, Jenny was still on the floor, now with a pillow over her face. She stirred when she heard the sound of a key in the lock. It was Sylvia.

"Sorry to barge in like this, kids, but I think I have some news that's worth interrupting whatever you're doing." She nearly tripped over Jenny.

"What are you doing down here?"

Jenny pulled the pillow off her face. "I fell out of my chair. Help me sit up, please. I'm fine — more pissed than anything else."

Sylvia helped Jenny up to the couch and sat beside her. "How long have you been on the floor? And where's Mark?"

"Long story short, we broke up, and I can't blame him. He's been frustrated for a long time, ever since we got to L.A. He's gone to Chicago to be part of a new theater company his old mentor is starting…Michael Kurkowitz. Have you ever heard of him?"

"Kurkowitz, that artsy-fartsy schmuck. Yeah, we've crossed paths."

"I should have seen it coming. Mark's been so distant, just going through the motions, like a robot. I'm afraid he'll start drinking again."

"You're too good for him. I saw it from the beginning, but I never said anything. 'Sylvia, keep your mouth shut,' I said, which for me is the supreme mitzvah. He doesn't deserve you."

"He deserves a lot better. I'm a screwed-up mess."

"Not so, sweetie. You're a hot property. That's why I came over here. I got a text from Lou Loring at CBS. She might have something for us, and I'm supposed to call her at two o'clock our time, which is…" She checks her watch. "…four minutes ago. Good, we don't want to seem too eager. I have her on Favorites."

As she scrolled to find Lou Loring, she held up two crossed fingers to Jenny.

"Hey, Lou, it's Sylvia. Sorry, I'm a little late. I couldn't get off a call from Oprah's P.A. Whaddaya got for me?... On the 14th?... Second guest?... Yeah, we'll be there. What time... Noon at the theater… Hey, thanks for this, Lou, you're my favorite lesbian… Aah, you're so sweet. See you in New York."

Sylvia turned to Jenny. "Dreams come true, sweetie. You got a guest spot on the Just Before Midnight show with Colby Ferrer. Next Wednesday. I'll book an early flight on Tuesday."

"That's super. My god, a late-night talk show. Thanks, Sylvia." They hugged, but Jenny suddenly broke out of the embrace. "I wish Mark could be with us. I wish my book were finished. I could be plugging it."

"That's OK, we'll get to that. As for Mark, well, it's his loss."

"You think I should call him?"

"Not now," Sylvia said. "It only makes you seem desperate."

"I am desperate," Jenny pleaded.

"Save it for later. A trip to New York is what you need now.

It'll clear your head. Can you be ready on Tuesday?"

"Yes, Rosie will help me. I can take her along, can't I?"

"Of course. I think we get a write-off for a caregiver."

"What about Debbie, your P.A.?"

"The budget doesn't stretch that far. Maybe I'll send her to Oxnard to check out the club scene. She can hang out with her brother. When's your caregiver getting here?"

"About an hour."

"OK, talk to her about coming every day. You can afford it. I gotta run. Tie up the loose ends. I'll send flowers and a bottle of Grey Goose to Annie Markus so she doesn't think we're running out on her —which we are, but them's the breaks."

Sylvia rushed out, leaving Jenny sitting alone.

The next night, Mark was at the Los Angeles International Airport, on his cell phone, talking to Michael Kurkowitz, and waiting to board his flight to Chicago.

"Michael, how's everything? I hope we're still on, 'cause I'm at LAX waiting for a red-eye to your most excellent Windy City… That's good, I'm excited, too. Can't wait to get started. Is Gina there? Yeah, go ahead, put her on speaker. Hi, Gina, looks like we'll be working together again…Lots of catching up to do. How's Philip….Oh, sorry about that…Same with me…Jenny and I ended it… Yeah, we can cry in our beer. I'll buy the beer…Yes…Uh-oh, gotta run, they're boarding my section…Me, too. See you soon." Mark clicked off, grabbed his suitcase, and hurried to board his flight.

The next day found Mark sitting at a large conference table with Michael Kurkowitz and Gina in Kurkowitz's theatre. Kurkowitz was warmer and more jovial than Mark expected. "Mark, we're so glad you're joining us."

"So glad," Gina echoed.

"Thanks, Michael. It's great to be here. I can't wait to get started," Mark said.

"You know Gina McDonald, of course."

"Yes, we've met," Mark said, trying to suppress a smile.

"Good. So, just to bring you up to fast —

"Up to speed," Gina cut in.

"Of course, 'speed,'" the director said, nodding at Gina. "Just to bring you up to speed, what we are creating here in Chicago is a center for artistic entertainment. We will bring together theatre, graphic arts, dance, music, slamming poetry —"

"He means poetry slams," Gina whispered to Mark.

"I get it," Mark whispered back.

Kurkowitz spread his arms wide. "All the expressive arts coming together. That's why I call it 'Le Grand Mélange.' And in Le Grande Mélange, we will be less concerned with creating new art — indeed, the artist who works from his freewheeling imagination is deluding himself."

"Or herself," Gina added.

"Of course," the director said. "The artist must not delude himself or herself about his originality. The artist is using a material that is already formed and so is only undertaking to elaborate on it."

"So, how does my play fit into all this?" Mark asked.

"Michael loves your play. Loves it," Gina assured him.

"Your play is the perfect vehicle for Le Grande Mélange," Kurkowitz continued. "Twenty-five actors and other artists have been working on it for over a year."

"A year? But I only sent it to you a month ago!" Mark exclaimed.

"Yes, yes, that's the beauty of Le Grande Mélange. It is a structured process that elaborates upon the material. The artists will use the found material — in this case, your play — and process it into the final work."

"But what's to process? My play is about a girl in Nebraska discovering family secrets."

"That's what your conception is now, but we are applying the process of Le Grande Mélange. What you have provided us with is a wonderful story arc. You must be very proud."

Kurkowitz shot up from his chair, grabbed Mark's hand, kissed him on both cheeks, shouted something in Polish, and scampered out of the room.

"He's quite a theatrical force, isn't he?" Gina said.

"That's putting it mildly," Mark said. "What's all this about a company of twenty-five rehearsing for a year?"

"Look, Hon, we've got to follow the guidelines of the municipal arts grant. The city requires that we keep at least twenty-five people employed over the course of the program. You'd be blown away by the level of talent. So, so creative and dedicated."

"That's great. But I guess my story of a Nebraska girl finding out about family skeletons gets reinterpreted."

Gina took both of his hands in hers. "It's for the greater good, darlin'. Local artists get work, Michael gets to do his thing, and you get an awesome credit for your resume. It will be great for you. And by the way how are you doing these days?"

"I'm OK. But now, I'm not sure about my play. How about you?"

"Working with Michael takes most of my energy, but I still have some left."

"For yoga, tennis, throwing pots?" he asked.

"You know that's not what I mean."

"Do you still hear from Phil?"

"Long gone," she snorted, "and good riddance, really. I finally realized what a narcissist he was."

She cocked her head and looked into his eyes seductively. "Mark, since you're going to be here, I thought maybe we could see where things might lead us."

"Yeah, 'the road not taken.' We had something going until... until we didn't."

"It takes two, hon. It takes two. It's been a long day. I'm starving, and you must be, too. My place is just across the street. Come on over, and I'll whip something up, and we can continue talking over there."

The conversation continued as they sat on the couch in Gina's apartment. On a tray between them was a TV remote, polished-off dinner plates, and two wine glasses with an empty bottle.

"Thanks, that was great. First wine I've had in a long time," he said.

"We killed the bottle. Should I open another?" she asked.

"Sure, why not? I can drown my sorrows. You sure are a genius with eggs and cheese."

"Just my signature omelet. Breakfast for dinner, remember?"

"Sure do. A life in the theatre on five dollars a day."

Gina gathered up the plates and glasses. "I'll just tidy up. Turn on the tube if you like."

"Thanks. There is something I want to watch."

Mark pointed the remote at the TV and clicked it on. He was just in time for Just Before Midnight, and he sat through Colby's opening monologue, twenty-or-so commercials, and the first guest, a politician promoting his new book written for children. Mark nodded off from the wine and jolted up in time to catch the end of Jenny's act.

Jenny was seated at her low mic. Compared to her usual attire, she was dressed very elegantly, just as Sylvia required.

"Stand-ups don't always have to look like someone dragged off the street," Sylvia told her. "This look will create a good contrast with your wheelchair."

"So, you like my wheels? I just had it customized. Put a Porsche emblem on the back. The guy at the dealership said he'd put me into a Porsche for just four-forty-nine a month. Such a deal. Before I got my emblem, I was just another hot chick in a wheelchair...I can't keep guys from hovering over me... Then, I realized they were just looking down my shirt. So, I got a marker and wrote on my boobs, 'These are not my eyes.' Didn't work. I'm thinking of wearing sunglasses over them... Go with the flow.... But one of the worst things about being in a wheelchair is having to talk to guys facing them below the belt…give me a break… At least crouch down so we can be face-to-face. I don't want that thing pointing at me. Thank you so much, you've been great!"

As the audience hooted and applauded, Colby Ferrer walked over to Jenny. He looked into the camera and smiled approvingly. "We have to take a break now, but stay with us, and we'll be right back...with more Jenny Corraggio!!

Mark was still staring at the TV when Gina came in from the bedroom and plopped down next to him. She meant her outfit to be provocative, and she succeeded — short, loose-fitting silk pajamas with a partially buttoned top. Even through the mist of wine, Mark was surprised when he saw her.

"I thought I'd get comfy. That OK?"

"Sure, yeah," he said with a hint of a smile.

"What are you watching?"

"Just Before Midnight. A friend's on it."

"Yeah, your ex. I could hear it from the bedroom. She looks good. Too bad about her accident. But she made lemonade out of lemons, right?"

"Yeah, lemonade. Tart...and sweet."

During the commercial break, two stagehands lifted Jenny in

her chair up to the platform where Ferrer was sitting at his desk. One of the men missed a step, and they nearly dropped Jenny.

"Don't worry, Jenny, this won't be on the tape," Ferrar assured her. Hearing his cue in his earpiece, he turned to the camera and announced, "All right, we're back with Jenny Corraggio."

He turned back to Jenny, who acted as if nothing had happened.

"So that's where your mother kept her stash? Good idea, that's where Robbie keeps his."

Ferrer called offstage to an unseen producer, "Right, Robbie?" He gave a thumbs-up to the unseen "Robbie," and turned back to Jenny.

"First of all, Jenny, congratulations on getting a one-hour special on Hulu." The audience applauded and shouted her name, and Jenny waved to thank them.

"I'm really excited. Can I wave to someone?" She waves to the camera. "Hi, dipshit. Hope you're having fun. Can I say 'dipshit' on late-night TV?"

"The censors will bleep it if we can't," Ferrer answered.

"I have a good friend in L.A. He's in Chicago now, but when we're together in L.A., it's the usual clash of careers."

Ferrer played along, "What does he do?"

"He has his own business in Beverly Hills. He cleans litter boxes for the rich and famous. We're both so busy that we don't get to see a lot of each other."

"So, he actually is a dipshit," Ferrer said. "Just so he doesn't bring his work home with him." Ferrer got the laugh he was fishing for.

"I wish he would. I worry about him spending so much time around rich, bored women and their pets. You know all the stories about women having flings with their cat-box man and then dumping him. It's a real kick in the butt."

"And pretty cheeky of them," Ferrer countered.

"At bottom, yes," she parried.

Ferrer turned to the camera. "Jenny Corraggio, everybody. Soon to be on Hulu. Coming up next, The Dry Heaves, so stay with us."

Mark pointed the remote at the television and clicked it off.

"She was good. Congratulations," Gina said.

"Thanks. She was damn good."

"The flame still flickers, eh?" Gina teased.

His focus remained on the blank television screen. "I don't know. But there is a twinge," he admitted.

"Come on, Mark. I know you too well. You're still hooked and won't admit it."

She leaned over and kissed his cheek. Mark continued to stare at the TV screen.

"I'm sorry. I'm coming on too strong," she said.

"You still look great, though. Too bad for Philip."

"Thanks, hon, but this won't work," she said. "We won't work, at least not now. So, let's just keep it professional."

Mark took her hand and kissed it. "Thanks for the omelet,"

he said. "But I think I need to get back to L.A. I'll go see Michael in the morning and say thanks, but no thanks. I'll take The Killer Diaries back with me and save it for a rainy day."

"Don't worry, you'll find a producer worthy of it." She stood up and mussed his hair. "Well, I'm beat. It's been a long day, and I'm going to bed. You're welcome to sleep on the couch."

"It won't be the first time," he said.

"You are still a shit, you know that?" They both laughed, and she disappeared into the bedroom.

Sylvia strode backstage to track down Colby Ferrer. She found him with a cocktail in one hand and reading something on a clipboard. "Mr. Ferrer, I want to thank you profusely for having us."

Ferrer continued reading. "Yeah, I hope you liked the show."

She extended her hand, with bracelets all a-clatter. "I'm Sylvia Mandelbaum, Jenny Corraggio's publicist and manager.

"Yeah, glad to meet you," Ferrer replied, finally looking up from the clipboard. "Here, hold my bourbon so I can shake your hand. That's quite a gal you've got there. Funny lady in a raunchily cute way. Kinda reminds me of myself when I was that age, except I wore braces and had a huge zit on the end of my nose. And I wasn't a girl."

"Jenny's not that young." Sylvia declared. "Beyond zits now, I can assure you. I'm hoping we can get another appearance on your show before too long."

Ferrer took back his bourbon.

"She'll have her own cable series by the end of the year." Sylvia fudged, hoping a contract from a cable network, still in negotiations, would be forthcoming.

"Then, we'll have to have her back. I'll speak with Lou Loring, who does our booking," he said, knowing he would assign the task to a P.A.

"I know Lou. She and I go way back."

"Well, then, I'm sure you'll be hearing from us again. Ciao."

Sylvia watched Ferrer walk away toward his dressing room. "I'll wait a few days and call Lou myself," she thought.

A week later, Jenny was back at her apartment in Los Angeles, sitting at the table, with a three-ring binder of her manuscript in front of her and a shredder next to her on the floor. Her hands shook as she pulled sheaves of pages out of the binder and ran them through the shredder. "Out...out...get out," she mumbled. At last, the shredding took its toll, and she leaned back in her chair to take a breather, which was interrupted by a knock at the door. It was Debbie.

"It's me, Debbie. Can I come in?"

Jenny straightened her hair and shirt, then wheeled over to the door and unlocked it. Debbie came in, carrying Sylvia's briefcase. She looked Jenny over apprehensively.

"You OK? Mom sent me over with the proofs of your publicity shots."

"Thanks. Let's take a look."

Debbie followed Jenny and saw pages scattered over the table.

"You cleaning up?"

"Just deleting parts of a former life," Jenny sighed.

Debbie put a sheet of proofs on the table.

"Mom circled the ones she likes best."

"She would, wouldn't she? Which do you like?"

Debbie pointed to one of the images. "This one and the one just below it. Mom's are too contrived."

"I agree with you," Jenny said. "This headshot and one with me in my chair. Let's go with these."

"Seriously?" Debbie was thrilled. "You agree with me?"

"Sure do."

"Thanks, that's a first for me…Hey, Mom told me about you and Mark. That really sucks."

"Well, it was for the best," Jenny said. "He wasn't happy, and I'm facing a whole new set of challenges."

"Yeah, but you must be hurting."

"I'll manage," Jenny said.

"Managing sucks," Debbie declared. "I know. Me and Tyler broke up two weeks ago, and it still hurts."

"I'm sorry. But you still have your dreams. How's the cannabis shop coming along? What were you going to call it?

"Get Potted. But that dream's dead now that we broke up. Tyler was the one with the connections and half the money. All I had were the names of people I met in rehab. They'd be customers. And we'd have my dad's matching funds, if we wrote a business plan…

What a sucky idea. He's such a dick…But that's OK, I got a better plan that'll work for just me. And screw Tyler."

Dissing the old boyfriend amused Jenny, and she played along. "Yeah, screw Tyler. Screw him good. What's the new idea?"

"Well," Debbie confided, "you know Mom sent me up to Oxnard to stay with my brother and check out the club scene. Oxnard's not that big, so I drove up and down the 101, up to Ventura, Thousand Oaks, Santa Barbara. And I got this idea. I hope you'll help me with it."

"Sure, Debbie, but I don't know how much help I can be."

"No, you're perfect for this…I want to do stand-up. Just like you."

Jenny was caught off guard and waited for Debbie's idea to sink in. "Well…I'm flattered…but…"

Debbie's excitement accelerated. "I know I can do it. I've always been a smart-ass, and I have loads of experience hanging out at bars…I mean, I know the bar scene, and I have friends who will let me perform. And I don't mean just on open mic nights. I can perform nights and work for Mom during the day until I catch a break."

"Yeah, like they say, 'Don't give up your day job.'"

"Don't worry, I won't. I doubt I can get anything out of my father. The cannabis shop was one thing, but he'll never go for bankrolling a stand-up comic."

"At least you won't need a business plan," Jenny teased. "But, I'm surprised. This is a hidden side to you, Deb. I'd like to help you, but I've never seen you perform. Why don't you work up some material, and we'll talk when you're ready."

"Hey, I'm all over it." Debbie reached into her back pocket and pulled out a wrinkled script. "I wrote this while I was at my brother's house. Will you listen to it?"

Jenny couldn't help but smile. "Sure, why not? Let's see what you got."

"Now, this is rough. But you'll get it."

Debbie grabbed a Diet Coke can from Jenny's table. "This will be the mic."

"Gotta have a mic."

She did a few stretches and shook her body to loosen up.

"Is this part of the act, or are you just getting yourself ready?"

"Just loosening up. I'd be doing this offstage before I come on."

"Good thought," Jenny responded.

Debbie squared her shoulders and launched into her routine.

"Hey, everybody, how's it goin'? It's so awesome to be back here in L.A. I've been traveling. Spent last week in Oxnard. Oxnard…now that's a name for a town. What do they call their high school mascot? The Snards? I was staying at my brother's house. Now, there's a real 'snard' for you, my brother. He's a vegan, juices everything. Drinks his breakfast every morning. I've been known to drink my breakfast, too. Also, lunch, dinner, and a midnight snack. Came out Bud-wiser for it.

One morning, I watched my brother throw kale into the

blender and chug it down. Have you ever tasted liquid kale? Nasty stuff. But I found out why. I was sitting on the back porch with coffee and a joint and looking out over his organic veggie garden. Pretty soon, the neighbor's dog comes over and pees all over his kale. Hey, it's all natural. How can it hurt?"

She looked at Jenny with uncertainty. "And that's as far as I got. But I've got some great lines on beets and cucumbers, too. From cucumbers, I go into a story about my boyfriend. What do you think?"

Jenny framed her words carefully. "You've got real possibilities. I love your delivery. You just need to work on the material. Tighten it up. I love the 'Snards' line but lose the 'Bud-wiser.' Will you be confident in front of an audience?"

"Are you kidding? In rehab, I spilled my guts in front of some very scary people. Playing a club will be a piece of cake. Besides —" She held out the Coke can. "I'll have a mic."

"Good girl," Jenny said, "but now I have to get back to work. Let's get together in a week or so, just you and me, and we'll see what you've come up with."

"Thanks, Jenny. But don't tell my mom."

Jenny made a "zip my lip" gesture.

Debbie waved the script to her. "I'll work real hard on this. You won't be disappointed," and she rushed out the door.

Jenny stretched, rubbed her neck, and wheeled over and transferred to the couch with the proof sheet. "'Bud-wiser,' ugh. But 'snards' is good. I like 'snards.' Mark would have liked 'snards.'"

Jenny heard a knock at the door. "Come on in; it's unlocked."

Mark opened the door slowly and stepped just inside. "You should keep it locked. You never know who's lurking outside."

Jenny was gobsmacked. "What? Why aren't you in Chicago?"

"Chicago was a bust."

She fumbled for a reply. "I'm sorry to hear that."

"I came back to get the rest of my stuff. That OK?"

"Sure. It's still in the bedroom.

"Thanks. You OK?" he asked tonelessly.

"Yeah…I'm fine. Where are you staying?"

"I got a place over on Melrose."

"Cool."

Mark pulled a dolly from out in the hall and wheeled it back into the bedroom. On his return, the dolly was piled with cartons and topped with clothes on hangers.

"Maybe I'll catch you at your next show," he said.

"That would be nice. Thanks."

Mark did not look back on his way out the door, pulling the dolly behind him.

Later that day at the apartment, Jenny waited on the phone to be connected to a receptionist. After several minutes of monotonous music, a voice came on the line.

"Uh, yes. My name is Jenny Corraggio. I'm a patient of Dr. Feinberg. He's ordered an MRI for me, and I'd like to make an appointment…C-O-R-R-A-G-G-I-O…"

She heard a knock at the door and shouted nervously for the knocker to wait a minute. She huddled over her phone and lowered her voice.

"Yes… Thursday, the twenty-ninth?... at 11:00? Nothing earlier?... Yes, of course, that would be fine…Thank you."

After she hung up, she shouted, "Come in!"

It was   Sylvia. "You on the phone? Who was it?" she asked, scoping out the room.

"Checking on my monthly Feinberg appointment. I forgot to record the time."

"You didn't return my call, so I thought I'd come over. How are the ribs?"

"Still sore. But Tylenol helps."

"You won't believe what Debbie is up to now." Her bracelets clattered as she spread her arms wide.

"Try me."

"She wants to be a stand-up comic. Can you believe it? Can't keep two thoughts together, and now she wants to do stand-up."

"Did she tell you about it?" Jenny asked.

"Nah, she doesn't tell me anything. But I found out. I have my sources. You know anything about this?"

"Well, actually, I do. She wants me to coach her," Jenny admitted.

"What, in your spare time? You're doing five shows a week, which we've cut back from ten, so you can work on your book, which we have to have ready for the release of your special. And now, you want to coach my daughter in her latest crazy? And, by the way," she added sarcastically, "how is the book coming along?"

Jenny exploded. "Don't get on my case. I'm not Debbie. The book is not coming along, if you want to know the truth."

"What? Writer's block? Look, if you take any longer, we'll have to get someone to ghostwrite it for you. But that means lots of long meetings, so you might as well write it yourself. You could talk it out on tape, and we can get it transcribed…or, no, you can get that app that goes from talk to type. Debbie told me about it."

"I can't talk it, either. I just can't concentrate." Jenny was at the point of tears.

"It's Mark, isn't it?"

"No, it's not Mark!"

"I was wrong about Mark," Sylvia said, trying to be calm. "He was good for you. You were good when he was around."

"Mark is over! Over and done with!"

"Look, maybe you two could get together…professionally, not romantically. Professionally. Maybe he didn't help directly, but… you know…he gave off a creative vibe that you picked up on."

"Mark is a whiner and a wimp. And easily manipulated. All Gina had to do was show some cleavage, and Markie-boy was off to the races. I don't need him…I've never needed him," she added with newly found venom in her voice.

"OK, I'm not saying you have to love him or even like him. He's back in L.A., and you'll be bumping into him. Just be cordial — you're an actress; you can do it. He doesn't have to come here.

You could meet for coffee so you could run things by him, just like before."

Jenny remained stone-cold.

Sylvia pressed further. "Look, Lucille Ball and Desi Arnaz. Desi was a womanizer and a shit, and Lucy knew it. But they found a way to work together, and they made millions."

"And their agents got a fat percentage," Jenny raged. "That's what it's all about, isn't it? Get Jenny and Mark back together, and Sylvia keeps getting her cut. I'm your meal ticket, Sylvia, aren't I?"

Wounded, Sylvia stared at Jenny for a moment before uttering, "I'm going to forget you said that. I'd better leave."

Sylvia was crying when she left the apartment.

"Now, what have I done?" Jenny asked herself. She picked up her laptop and flung it at the door, screaming, "Mark, you son of a bitch!"

The next morning, the apartment seemed to be just as it was when Sylvia left, except for a glass and a half-empty bottle of vodka on the table. Total silence, until a key rattled in the lock, and Debbie let herself in. "Jenny, are you here? Everything OK?"

Debbie picked up the laptop and put it back on the table. She picked up the vodka bottle and checked to see how much was gone.

Jenny wheeled in from the bedroom, red-eyed and disheveled.

"I used Mom's key and let myself in. Are you OK?" Jenny asked.

"Never better. Except for my ribs, my head, and my conscience."

Debbie pointed at the vodka bottle. "Drowning your sorrows?"

"No, they're floating right there on the surface, doing the backstroke."

"I could have told you this stuff never works. Mom says you're pissed at her."

"She should be pissed at me. I said some very unkind things to her last night, which she didn't deserve. Your mother has been so good to me, and I need to apologize and ask… no, beg…for forgiveness. And I will, as soon as I get my head together." She looked at the bottle and shuddered. "What's up with you? She didn't send you over here, did she?"

Debbie pulled a sheaf of folded papers from her pocket. "No, I didn't tell her I was coming. I finished my routine, but this probably isn't the time to show it to you."

"You're right." Jenny massaged her temples with both thumbs. "This morning, nothing is funny, and it wouldn't be fair to you."

She jumped when she heard a knock at the door. "Oh, Jesus, it's Sylvia. Time to face the music." She steeled herself for the meeting and called out, "Sylvia, I'm so sorry. Please…come in."

Mark opened the door and looked around the room. "Sorry, I didn't know you had company."

The apartment was the last place Debbie wanted to be. She dashed to the door and garbled, "Jenny, I gotta go. Hi, Mark, nice to see you. I dropped off a script, and I'll leave you guys to catch up."

She left without closing the door, so Mark pushed it shut. He and Jenny stared at each other until Mark broke the silence.

"I miss you."

"I miss you, too. Sorry. I've been drinking," she said.

"So have I. Can we talk?"

"Yes, why don't you tell me about Chicago?"

"Disaster," he said. "A pure, unmitigated disaster. I didn't see Kurkowitz being such a lunatic. I guess I forgot how he could be. And with Gina McDonald being his second-in-command, it was just too awkward. I stayed at her place overnight — on the couch, I promise you. But I did fall off the wagon with two bottles of Sauvignon Blanc."

"Was it good? The wine, I mean"

"Not worth it. I threw up in the middle of the night. So, the next morning, I went to Michael and apologized and told him I couldn't join the company. He was pissed, of course, and started yelling at me in Polish. I guess I burned a bridge, but I don't care… Jen, is it OK if I come back?

"But haven't things changed for you?" she asked.

"Look, I made a big mistake. I know I'm the one who left, but I really want to be here…with you."

"You're sure about that?"

"I'm absolutely sure," he said. "Once I got to Chicago, I started having second thoughts about leaving you. One full day with Kurkowitz and Gina was enough. The grass wasn't greener. I have to stop feeling sorry for myself and get back to those script ideas

I've been shoving back in a drawer. As soon as I landed in L.A., I got cold feet… I needed some time to work up the courage to face you. That's when I found out you were still in New York. I couldn't come back here, so I got my own place. With a roommate — a male roommate."

"What streaming services do you have?" she asked.

"I don't know…what difference does it make?

"Just asking," she replied with feigned innocence.

"You're messing with me now, aren't you?" Mark realized she was teasing him and began to chuckle." Now, where was I? Oh, right…When I was in Chicago, I caught you on the Ferrer show. You were fantastic. I think he loved going head-to-head with you… Look, I'm not here to flatter you or talk shop. Will you let me come back? Hell, I'll even go back to Whiplash Films if they'll take me."

"Why would you want to come back? I'm a mess. I'm a fucked-up cripple who can't walk, can't pee right, and is deathly afraid of bed sores."

Mark went to her, and they caught each other in a long and warm embrace.

"I couldn't leave you," he whispered.

"I don't want to be left. You know that, don't you?"

"I wish I had your guts," he said.

"Guts? Is that what you call it? Underneath it all, I'm terrified."

"But you make it work for you. You showed it on the Ferrer

show."

"That's just my shtick, staying out in the lights so I can keep the shadows away for a while."

"Well, you were glowing that night. But what took you so long to get back to L.A.? Did Sylvia get you another gig? I thought you were flying back the next day."

"We were, but I had a little accident. Transferring from my wheelchair into the taxi, I slipped off my chair and missed the taxi seat. I fell into the gutter and bruised my ribs."

"What?" Mark was flabbergasted.

"The cabbie was mortified. He knelt down and prayed while Sylvia called 9-1-1. The EMTs let Sylvia and Rosie ride in the ambulance with me."

"Are you OK? Your ribs, I mean?"

"They're fine, just sore…but they found something else."

"You're pregnant?"

"Geez, how I wish. No, sweetie, they did MRIs and CAT scans. And here's the part where you're welcome to walk right back out that door."

Mark braced himself for what was coming next. "What are you talking about?"

"Seems that ever since I fell off the ladder, my spine has been deteriorating. So, in eighteen months…two years…I won't be able to sit up. I'll be flat on my back from then on."

Mark stood up shakily and walked to the farthest corner of the room. "Oh, my god," he said.

"That's what I said. Looks like that'll be the end of my act. It's hard enough for an audience to accept wisecracks from me sitting in my wheelchair. But it won't work when I'm pushed onstage lying on a gurney."

"Stop it, Jen. If your spine gives out — and I say if — you're not going to lose your talent. Now's the time to get back to that goddamn book of yours. I'll help you . . .I'll prod you. . .I'll be relentless."

"You don't mean that. I can't let you," she pleaded.

"I'm serious," he said. "Does Sylvia know about this?"

"Not about the spine problem. Anyway, I need to call her and apologize for the nasty things I said to her. I was a real bitch again."

"Get on the phone and say what you have to. Tell her you need a couple of weeks to rest, then it's full steam ahead. When do you start shooting your special?"

"Seven or eight weeks, I can't remember."

"Perfect," Mark exclaimed. "You'll be there, and with a finished manuscript."

Jenny flashed a grin. "Oooh, I love it when you take charge. Makes me hot."

Mark rushed over to her and pulled her up out of her chair and caught her in a strong embrace. As they pressed their lips together, Jenny slipped through his arms and ended up on the floor.

"Oh, my god. Are you all right? I'm so sorry."

Jenny looked up at him and winced. "I'm OK. Damn legs let me down, so to speak."

Mark panicked and said he'd call 9-1-1.

"No, don't. I'm OK. This is what happened in the taxi." She took a few deep breaths. "Just let me rest here for a while."

"What can I get you? A pillow? Pain pills?"

"I'm good," she said. "You get a different perspective from down here. I think I can use it in my act —you know, lying on my back, I could look up skirts. It's a whole new bit for the cable show — 'Underpants of the Stars.' We could call it 'Thongs and Things.'"

"Lemonade out of lemons," he said. "I sure love you."

She took one more deep breath and asked Mark to sit her up. "Then, we'll figure out how to get me back in my chair."

Mark pulled her into a sitting position with her back against the couch and sat on the floor next to her.

"I really need to call Sylvia." But she stopped herself and smiled mischievously at Mark. "But, not right now." She linked an arm with his. "What a life, huh? I coulda been a contendah."

"You ain't no contendah, Kid," he replied. "You da champ."

THE GIRL WITH THE TOPAZ RING

Josh Tanner figured his father never loved him. The Old Man left Josh's mother right after he was born. Although he knew where his father lived, Josh never heard from him, except for the occasional one-hundred-dollar birthday check and a card for his high school graduation. There was nothing in the "Congratulations, Graduate" card but the check and his father's signature, "Frederick G. Williamson." Not "Dad," or even "Fred," but the full signature.

Josh's mother died giving birth to him, and he was raised by his grandparents, Lois and Ben Tanner. Josh tried contacting his father several times, but no answer ever came. He thought of visiting after the graduation card, but it was too far and very expensive to get from San Francisco to Houston. Besides, he was saving his money for college.

Working part-time at a radio station, Josh needed six years to get through San Francisco State. The day he graduated, at age 24, another card arrived. Inside were six crisp one-hundred-dollar bills and, again, the full signature. Scrawled opposite the printed Hallmark piffle read:

I need to see you. Come ASAP. Fly and rent a car.

Drawn by equal parts anger and curiosity, Josh was on a plane to Houston the next morning.

Josh pulled out of the rental car lot and told Siri the address his father had scrawled on the back of the envelope. He headed north from the airport on a narrow road that threaded along a winding bayou. In half an hour, Siri told him to turn right onto Wintergate Drive, and that "238" would be on the left.

The house lay back from the road, nearly hidden behind a grove of tall pines. Josh turned into the circular driveway and stopped behind an old green Jaguar parked out front. No one seemed to be around as he trudged up the gravel walk past the two stone lions to the front door. He pushed aside a cascade of ivy to find the doorbell.

Footsteps inside grew louder, and the door opened. A woman blinked in the sunlight. She was tall with blonde hair pulled back into a ponytail. Josh figured her to be in her mid–fifties.

"I guess you're Josh."

"Yes, I'm here to see my father."

"I'm Elise. Come on in."

She shut the door behind them and motioned for Josh to go into the living room. The walls were hung with paintings, mostly landscapes, giving the room the look and feel of an art gallery. In a corner, next to a window, a cockatoo in a brass cage ruffled its feathers and squawked at him. Dominating the room was a full-size grand piano with a stack of sheet music resting on its closed lid.

Josh felt as if random puzzle pieces about his father had appeared: the paintings, a piano, a bird.

"Sit down while I get my coat," Elise said. On her way out into the hall, she called over her shoulder, "The cockatoo's name is Alexander, and your father did the paintings."

"Where is he?" Josh asked.

Elise returned, slipping into a pink jacket.

"Your father is in the hospital. The ICU. He's been ill for several weeks, and now he's failing, but he told me to bring you right away. We can take my car."

"What's wrong with him?"

"He's old. He's 82. What can I say?"

Elise floored the Jag as she turned down the bayou road. Josh saw her as an attractive woman, but not one to be messed with. She was not wearing a wedding ring.

"You a friend of my father?"

"A longtime friend. And in case you're wondering, a friend with benefits. Now, I'm his caregiver."

"Lucky man."

Elise pulled the Jag into a handicap space next to the hospital entrance. She stretched across Josh's lap to open the glove box and pull out a red handicap placard. Josh felt her cheek brush his chest. "Is this a test?" he asked himself.

Elise hung the placard on the mirror, flipped her ponytail out of her collar, and got out. Josh followed her into the hospital and over to a bank of elevators.

It was the first time Josh had ever seen the man who fathered him, now a withered husk hooked up to a machine by an array of tubes and wires. Straw-colored wisps stuck out from each side of his otherwise bald head.

"Hello, Frederick. I'm Josh." Josh could not bring himself to call this gaunt scarecrow Dad.

Josh did not flinch as his progenitor stared into his eyes. The old man motioned to the tray table beside the bed, which made Elise spring to life and retrieve the white envelope leaning against the pink water pitcher.

"He wants you to have this," Elise whispered as she thrust the envelope at Josh.

Only then did Josh disengage his eyes from his father's stare. The envelope was not sealed, and he pulled out a color photograph of a red-haired young woman posing in her graduation cap and gown — high school or college, he could not tell.

The old man raised a hand and bent two fingers toward himself.

"He wants to say something to you," Elise said.

Josh stepped forward and leaned in close to the old man, who smelled of disinfectant and cologne. The strength of the old man's voice surprised him as his father pointed to the photo.

"You have a sister," he said.

"A sister," Josh repeated, as a wave of disbelief passed over him, followed by the sobering thought that nothing this old man did should be surprising. Josh whispered his father's name, but the old man fell back asleep. A nurse came in and waved Josh and Elise away. They walked down the hall to the visitors' lounge and sat opposite each other on chairs covered in green faux leather.

Josh waved the photo toward Elise. "You know anything

about this?"

"First time I heard of her. And she's not mine, if that's what you're thinking. I have two boys. One's in the Army and the other drives for UPS."

Josh examined the photo. The girl wore a blue graduation cap and gown. The yellow tassel on the cap contrasted with the curly red hair that fell to her shoulders. She held a rolled-up paper in her left hand, obviously a diploma. She wore a walking boot on her right foot.

"Broken ankle? Broken foot? Skiing in Vail? Switzerland?" he puzzled.

She wore a ring with a yellow stone on her left middle finger.

"Elise, what kind of gemstone is yellow?"

"Topaz. It's my birthstone. November." She grinned at him. "But don't ask me the year."

Josh handed her the photo.

"Any idea who this might be?"

"Not a clue. Pretty, though."

Josh took back the photo and stood up.

"I'm going back in there to see if he can explain this."

Josh walked back down the hall to his father's room with Elise following. The nurse appeared at the door. The look on her face told them all they needed to know.

Josh stood at the foot of his father's bed. The tubing and oxygen mask had been removed. Josh was sure he saw his father's face frozen into a smirk.

"You old bastard," Josh thought. "You were never a part of my life, and now you leave me with a sister as a goodbye gift."

"He looks peaceful," Elise said.

"No, he doesn't."

"You're right, she admitted, "Just smug, as usual. If you're worried about the funeral arrangements, he had everything planned out. He wants to be buried in the back garden under the live oak tree. I can show you the spot."

"I'll pass."

Josh and Elise hardly spoke as she drove him back to the house, except for the Caregiver-with-Benefits mentioning the will.

"He promised me the house, but the rest of the assets will probably go to you," she said.

"I don't want anything from him," Josh spat out, but immediately felt ashamed of his own rancor.

"I can understand how you feel," Elise said in a motherly tone. "But he did give you a sister."

"A half-sister, you mean."

They continued to drive in silence until Elise broke through. "Aren't you curious?"

"Yeah, I am. I really am," he replied.

"Wish I could help, but I only found out about this child last week. Let me know if you find her," she said. After more silence, she asked him about his flight back to San Francisco.

"Tomorrow at noon."

"Why don't you stay over? You can have your choice of guest

rooms."

Josh remained silent, thinking of his father grinning from his grave under the oak tree.

"What about it?" Elise asked in a tone bordering on the confrontational.

"I was planning to stay in a hotel near the airport." Josh calculated that he'd save money, which was always in short supply, if he took her up on her offer.

"OK, thanks," he said," then I'll leave early in the morning."

"Good," she said. "Now, let's get something to eat. There's a good ol' Texas barbecue joint on the way."
Elise and Josh sat at one of the newspaper-covered tables at Gunny's Rib Shack and confronted a huge plate of ribs, to be washed down with longneck bottles of Shiner beer, which Elise assured was a local favorite.

Josh asked her how she came to work for his father.

"Answered an ad in the paper," she said, delicately placing a cleaned rib bone at the side of her plate.

"I showed up at the house, and we hit it off real well. That was twenty-one years ago."

"Your children, what about them?"

"Their dad got custody after the divorce, and he took them to Colorado when he moved."

Josh was about to ask Elise why her ex-husband got custody but ultimately decided he didn't need to go down that path and changed the subject.

"What about the piano? Do you play?"

"No," she replied wistfully. "Fred did. Mostly classical. He'd come in from the back deck, where he worked on his paintings and would sit down and play. After he got too weak and needed a wheelchair, he stopped playing. But he kept on painting."

"That house is pretty big for just you and my dad," he said.

"He told me he bought it during a foreclosure. Couldn't pass up a bargain."

Elise leaned toward him and lowered her voice. "You're not upset about him leaving the house to me, are you?"

"Not in the least."

Elise took a swig from her longneck. "You could move here, and we could turn it into a bed and breakfast. Each bedroom has its own private bath. It used to be a brothel."

Josh chuckled at the idea of his father living in a former house of ill repute.

"Seriously," she said. "We could be partners."

"You mean, I'd move here from San Francisco?"

"Why not?" she asked. "You're your father's son, and he and I hit it off real well. No reason you and I couldn't as well."

Josh did his best to look unfazed by what sounded like a crazy idea while Elise pressed on.

"We could —" Elise interrupted her thought, leaned back in her chair, and gave him a knowing look. "Oh, I see. You have a girlfriend."

"Not at the moment," he replied.

"See, then you're unencumbered."

Josh looked down at his plate and moved a rib bone around in a puddle of sauce.

"Thanks for the offer, but this will have to be your project."

Then Josh gave her a wink. "Maybe you could restore the place to its former glory."

Elise laughed. "Back to a brothel? Well, I am in good with the sheriff."

"There you go then," he said.

Elise reached over and patted his hand. "But only if you stick around to play the piano."

The sun was going down when they got back to the house. The guardian lions glowed in the fading light, and Josh's fingers were still sticky from the sauce on the ribs.

He said the day had taken its toll and begged off watching TV with her. Elise escorted him upstairs to one of the bedrooms. She advised him that if he needed anything, she'd be down the hall. He said goodnight and quickly closed the door behind him. He listened to her footsteps fading away.

Josh took a quick shower and changed into the running shorts and Grateful Dead T-shirt he always slept in. He noticed that the walls were lined with more of his father's paintings, all landscapes with lush tropical greenery. He examined the largest one and discovered a woman's face behind one of the palm fronds. He moved on down the line of paintings and found that each of them showed the same dark-haired woman partially hidden in the greenery. One showed her neck and shoulders; in another, he could see a brightly colored shawl extending down to her waist. In the painting closest to the bed, the woman was leaning against a vine-covered tree trunk, her head turned and looking off to her left. The shawl had slipped off her right shoulder, revealing a creamy white breast.

"I wonder what the old man called this one, 'Jane of the Jungle'?" he thought.

As soon as Josh jumped into bed, he heard footsteps coming down the hall, then a knock at the door.

"Everything all right in there?" — it was Elise.

"Yeah, fine, thanks. Good night."

"Just checking," she said from the other side of the door.

"I'm good. See you in the morning."

Josh listened as her footsteps faded back down the hall. He let out a long breath and wondered why Elise came to check on him. What would she be wearing? A quilted robe and fuzzy slippers? A naughty outfit from the Victoria's Secret catalogue? Or nothing, like the woman in the painting? He was relieved that his father's "beneficial friend" went back to her room.

On the plane ride back to San Francisco, Josh further examined the photo of the girl with the topaz ring, the girl who was supposedly his half-sister.

"You did it, Old Man, you've hooked me into hunting for her," he thought, "and I know where I'm going to start."

Josh had no sooner dumped his duffel at his apartment when his cell phone buzzed. It was his grandfather inviting him over for dinner, so he could tell them about his trip to Houston.

Josh was surprised that his grandparents would want to hear about Fred Williamson, the man who fathered him, but ran off as soon as he was born.

That his mother had died birthing Josh endeared his grandparents even less to Williamson. But curiosity usually trumps bitterness, so of course Lois and Ben would want all the details.

Josh tucked the photo of the red-haired girl into his jacket, ran a comb through his curly brown mop, and ran down the steps to where he had squeezed his nondescript Toyota into a space just inches from the No Parking zone. He crossed the Bay Bridge and headed north to his grandparents' house in El Cerrito.

Grandma Lois had the table already set for the three of them. At each place was her signature salad, a square of lime Jello infused with grated carrot and topped with a dollop of Miracle Whip.

His grandfather was already seated at the table, reading the Chronicle's sports page when Josh walked in. Lois hovered between the dining room and the kitchen. Josh could tell she was nervous, a state that was confirmed by the sound of a dish crashing to the kitchen floor.

Lois brought in plates of roast beef, mashed potatoes, and green beans. Ben asked how his trip went.

"Fine. It was fine." Josh kept his eyes on his plate. The roast beef was tender. The three of them concentrated on their food, with

Josh pausing only to congratulate his grandmother on her culinary abilities. His grandfather broke the silence.

"Tell us about it," he said.

"The trip?" Josh asked, unable to avoid playing coy.

"Yes, we want to know," Lois chimed in.

"No, you don't," Josh thought to himself.

He wondered if he should let them tiptoe around the elephant in the room that was his father or just come out with it.

He just came out with it.

"When I got there, Frederick Williamson, my father, was in the hospital. ICU. He died before he could say much."

Josh was sure his grandmother breathed a sigh of relief. Ben leaned forward, pushing his shirt cuff into his gravy-laden mashed potatoes.

"I'm sorry," Ben said. "You know how we feel – felt – about him, but he was your father after all."

Lois remained stone-faced.

"Don't worry. I'm not shedding any tears over the man who was never part of my life, except for the birthday cards he sent me."

Josh told himself it was time to get on with it, even though dessert hadn't shown up yet. "And then, there's this." Josh pulled the photo out of his pocket and waved it toward them. "He gave it to me just before he died."

Lois took the photo and adjusted her glasses. As soon as the red-haired girl came into focus, Lois inhaled sharply and handed the photo to Ben.

"Funniest thing," Josh said. His last words to me were 'you have a sister.'"

Ben sat back, dragging a line of gravy over the tablecloth as he stared at the photo. Lois sprang into the kind of action that is motivated by avoidance.

"I'll clear up," she said. "You two go into the living room. And I'll bring out your pie and coffee."

Ben jerked his head toward the left, and Josh followed him into the living room. They sat in the two worn-out chairs facing the giant flatscreen hanging above the fireplace. On the mantel, for as long as Josh could remember, was a framed photo of a teenage girl, his mother, Jeanette. Ever since he turned twenty-three, he regarded the photo with an extra measure of sadness as he realized he had become older than his mother would ever be.

"Gramps, is there something I should know?"

Ben held the photo gently, one corner between thumb and finger.

"Yes, there is, I suppose. Let me tell you about it before your grandmother comes in. It's not something she has ever wanted to dwell on."

Josh shifted toward the older man. "OK, tell me, please."

"Yes, you do have a sister, a half-sister. It's something we never wanted to talk about. This could be her. But how your father came to know about her, I don't know."

He gave the photo a gentle tap.

"She probably does have red hair like this girl."

"Probably?" Josh whispered.

"I've never seen her, and I have no idea where she is. She's five years older than you, that's all I know. You see, your mother was in high school, her junior year. She was going steady with the captain of the football team. She was beautiful, and the two of them seemed like the ideal all-American couple. You see where this is going, don't you?"

"Yeah, please go on."

"He was the quarterback, and he had red hair. One thing led to another, and your mother got pregnant. They were too young, and they both wanted to go to college, so your mother decided to have the baby and give it up for adoption. Your Grandmother took her up to your Aunt Judy's in Oregon, and they stayed there until the baby was born. We told everyone that Jeanette was going through a breakdown and needed therapy."

"So, mental illness is more forgivable than having a baby?" Josh asked. He felt immediately ashamed for making such a sarcastic comment.

"Your mother felt it was more forgivable than giving away a child."

Ben rubbed his eyes, and Josh could see a tear forming.

"Your mother came home, and by that time, Bill Leffler — that was her boyfriend — was off to college back East. They never had any contact after that. She graduated from high school and got into Berkeley. Yes, pretty and smart, and she would have been proud of you."

Josh felt tears flowing from his own eyes as he gazed at the photo of his mother atop the mantel.

"Your mother met Fred Williamson on a geology field trip. He was a visiting lecturer. She thought he was the one, and Lois and I did, too. But, as soon as he found out she was 'with child' as they say, he skedaddled. Last we heard, he was in South America with an oil company."

"So, that's how he made his money," Josh said.

"I guess so, but your mother was determined to get on with her life without him, and with you. But the Lord had other ideas. He took Jeanette and left you in her place.

Ben looked Josh in the eyes. "You are your mother's boy, and we couldn't be prouder." The two men sat in silence as Lois rumbled around in the kitchen.

"I wonder when that pie is coming," said Ben.

Josh cleared his throat. "So, my mother had a child who would be my half-sister. Well, thank god, Frederick wasn't her father, too."

"I have to agree with that," Ben said.

"And you have no idea where the red-haired girl in the cap and gown might be? Look at the photo. I'm told that the ring she's wearing is topaz. Does that mean anything to you?"

"I wish it did," Ben said, turning away from his grandson's gaze.

"Please, help me here, Pops. She's my mother's child, your and Grandma's granddaughter.

Josh's voice cracked in desperation. "Forget all the half-sister rigamarole; she's my sister, my blood. I have to find her."

"Let me talk with your grandma. It'll be hard for her, dredging up those old memories, but she'll come around." Ben leaned over and hugged his grandson.

"This is important for all of us, Sonny Boy. We'll help you any way we can."

As he drove back to San Francisco, Josh pondered all that his grandfather had told him. What happened to the red-haired quarterback who got his mother pregnant? Did his mother really love Frederick Williamson, the man who had fathered him?

"Did she get to see me, to hold me before she died?"

And hovering over all his thoughts — where was his sister?

The next day at the radio station, Josh could hardly concentrate on his job, editing raw news copy into two-minute segments to be read on air every quarter hour. A quote from a Senator calling his opponents' claims "a red herring" sent Josh into a reverie about red hair. He was always up against a time crunch, and he pulled himself back to the Senator before he lost another precious second.

Josh got a break at noon when the station carried an hour of news and talk from the network feed. On his way to the break room to pull his tuna sandwich out of the fridge, he walked past the office where his coworker Sarah was crouched in front of a pair of computer monitors.

The thought flashed before him that Sarah, a computer geek with a Mariana Trench of research knowledge, might be able to help him in his search.

Josh and Sarah weren't close. Although Josh considered her cute, she was the station's IT whiz and, in her spare time, a gamer. Josh had gone to lunch with her once, and she spent the whole 50 minutes recounting, between bites of quinoa and tofu, the plots of a half dozen episodes of Dr. Who. Josh loved film noir and definitely was not a vegan, so the lunch generated zero sparks.

"This is purely business," Josh thought as he popped into Sarah's office. She was glued to a screen, sipping a kombucha.

"Hey, Sarah, I forgot my lunch and was going across the street to the deli. You want to come with?"

Straw still in mouth, Sarah sucked in the last of her kombucha with a gurgle.

"Sure. I need a break. These screens are starting to make my eyes cross."

They ordered at the counter and sat at the only remaining table. Sarah ordered the veggie bowl. Josh did the same, although he really wanted a pastrami on rye. He figured he should start to get on Sarah's good side, foodwise.

Josh asked Sarah if she could help him with a project he was doing "for a friend." He wasn't ready to disclose anything about his family secret.

"My friend wants to track down a student who graduated from Los Osos High School in 2013 or '14, Bill Leffler. He played quarterback and went back East on a scholarship. Don't know if it was athletic or academic. For what it's worth, my friend said Leffler had red hair."

"Sounds like fun," Sarah said. "Who's your friend?"

"Can't say."

"Hey, two mysteries for the price of one." Sarah stabbed at a chunk of avocado. Why don't you go to Los Osos High School yourself and look this guy up?"

"I figured you could do that. But what we really want to know is where Bill Leffler is now and what he's doing."

Josh figured he'd start Sarah off chasing down the red-haired quarterback before he eased her into the search for his sister.

"I'm willing to pay you for your trouble," Josh said. "I've got — "He caught himself and rephrased. "I've been given a budget."

Sarah smiled at him. "I said this sounds like fun. You only have to pay me if it starts to get boring.

Josh was sitting at his editor's desk when he felt a tap on his shoulder. He turned and came nose-to-nose with Sarah.

"Follow me," she whispered and walked out into the hall.

Josh followed her down into her office. She closed the door and turned to him.

"Dead end, Dude. I tracked Leffler, your red-haired quarterback, to college back East. Went to Dartmouth but never got to play football. He crashed his motorcycle into a tree, wasn't wearing a helmet, died instantly."

"The guy just wouldn't wear protection," Josh thought. With this lead gone, he realized he'd have to open up to Sarah with the whole story.

"Where do we go now?" she asked.

Josh liked the sound of the word we. "Sounds like she's into this. That's good," he thought.

"You got a minute to hear me on company time?" he asked.

"The door's shut, and I'm not screaming, so HR won't care."

"OK," he said. "There's more to this than I first told you."

"I guessed that from the get-go," she said. "You're not much of a liar with this red-haired quarterback story. I figured there's more to it. And, by the way, don't ever say you're asking for a friend when it's you who wants the answer. 'For a friend' is the lamest cover-up of all."

"Guilty," Josh admitted. "That's why you're a researcher, and I'm a dumb shmuck."

"But a nice shmuck."

"Thanks." Josh couldn't help smiling. "Well, here's the story. Yes, I'm the one who's looking for someone. The quarterback was only what I thought would be a first step."

Josh pulled the photo out of the pouch of his hoodie and handed it to Sarah.

"I'm looking for her. She's my sister, my half-sister, actually."

Sarah peered at the photo for what felt like eternity to Josh before she raised her eyes to him.

"She's got red hair, just like the quarterback, who was probably seventeen years old. I'm guessing he's the father. And since you don't have red hair, I figure he's not your father."

She looked at the photo again.

"So, why don't you ask your mother?"

"My mother's dead. Died giving birth to me. I guess I should feel guilty, but I don't. Just empty."

"I'm sorry. What about your father?"

"He died recently. Never was part of my life. That's how I got this photo, kind of a deathbed bequest. The last thing he said to me was, 'You have a sister.' My curiosity is eating me alive, and I've got to find her, talk to her."

"So, you're an orphan now?"

"Not really. I have my grandparents."

"Welcome to the club. Me, too. Foster parents. They were old when they took me in, and now they're even older. They live in Marin. Nice people, but I don't see them much now. You have other siblings?"

Josh chuckled. "Not that I know of, but who knows what my father was up to over the years. That's why I want to find the only sister — OK, half-sister — that I have."

"How old do you think she'd be?"

"Four or five years older than me. Close to thirty."

"The cap and gown," Sarah said. "High school or college?".

"I'm sure it's college. She looks too old for high school."

"Any idea what college?"

"Not a clue."

"Very cool. This is the kind of research that turns me on."

Sarah's eyes widened in excitement,

"And you're lucky," she said. "I don't think this will be boring, so there's no charge. But you can take me to dinner sometime."

That night, before he fell asleep, Josh thought about Sarah Coughlin. He found her enthusiasm attractive, unlike the aloof computer nerd he'd always considered her to be. And a lot more attractive, even under her baggy sweats and hair twisted into a topknot, like the ballet dancers that his friend Will referred to as bunheads. He doubted Sarah Coughlin was into ballet.

The next day, after work, Josh drove out to his grandparents' house. His grandfather had gone fishing, which gave him the opportunity to talk with his grandmother alone. They sat in the kitchen over cups of coffee.

Josh could see that Lois was nervous. He didn't mind when she asked her inevitable question, "Have you found anyone yet?" He knew what she meant. This was her probe into the state of his love life. His standard response was to say he was "working on it" before changing the subject. This time, he threw her a bone.

"Well, there is this girl at the station who's piqued my interest. But it's too early to say anything."

"What's her name?"

"Sarah."

"That's nice."

Josh did not respond. He stared at the swaying tail of the cat clock above the sink.

Lois broke the silence by apologizing for becoming upset at the sight of the girl wearing the topaz ring.

"It brought back so many terrible memories of your mother and that baby. But it was the ring that shocked me."

Josh looked into her eyes, but remained silent, hoping his look would nudge her into continuing, which she did.

"We gave your mother that ring for her sixteenth birthday. The only time she took it off was when she gave it to the nurse and asked her to make sure it would stay with the baby."

Lois began sobbing, and tears rolled down her cheeks, and she was barely able to choke out her next words.

"I'm sure that girl is my granddaughter."

"And I intend to find her," Josh whispered.

Josh went over and hugged his grandmother for a long moment, then turned and walked to the kitchen doorway.

"I love you, Grandma," he said, his voice cracking as he turned and left Lois alone with her memories.

On the drive back into San Francisco, Josh wiped away his own tears and mentally kicked himself for not staying longer with his grandmother. But he convinced himself that lingering would only have increased the elderly woman's pain.

The next morning at work, he popped his head into Sarah's office, but she was not there. As he started back down the hall, Sarah came out of the elevator and ran toward him. She flashed past him and nearly dropped the sheaf of files she cradled against her bosom.

"Can't talk now. I'm late and have to finish this. Come back in fifteen."

Josh sat down at his desk and checked the time on his computer screen. 7:43. Did she know something? The fifteen minutes dragged on as he looked for little tasks to pass the time. He had never organized paper clips by size and color before.

At 7:58, Josh bolted out of his chair and down to Sarah's office.

"Just in time. I'm done," Sarah said.

"You find out something?" Josh asked a little too loudly. He looked out into the hall to see if anyone could have heard him and then carefully closed the door.

Sarah smiled at him, and he thought he saw a twinkle in her eye that signaled success. "I did, but it took a while," she answered. "I spent a couple of hours diving deep into a Google rabbit hole. You know how one thing leads to another. I found a newspaper story in a local Michigan paper from thirty years ago. It was about a couple who had adopted a baby."

Josh felt a door slam on his hopes. "A lot of people adopted babies thirty years ago."

"Yes, but this baby came with a tiny gold bracelet with an adult-size ring attached to it. A topaz ring."

Josh felt his heart pound as he reached for the words. "In Michigan? Where in Michigan?"

"Kalamazoo. The couple's name is Larson. Janet and Phil."

Josh looked at her in disbelief.

"My sister was adopted in Oregon by a couple from Michigan?"

"People come from all over to adopt. Think of the parents of kids from Korea. Or Siberia. I tried contacting the Kalamazoo Records office, but they are closed for the weekend. I'll try again Monday."

Josh reached out and hugged Sarah and planted a kiss squarely on the bun on top of her head.

"Sarah, you are truly Wonder Woman."

Sarah slowly pulled away from him. She smiled and straightened her hair.

"Glad you think so. Now, how about that dinner you promised?"

Josh drove to the address Sarah gave him. Her apartment was on Potrero Hill between Gonzo's Pizza and the Get Potted cannabis shop. He circled the block, looking for a parking place, and on his third time around, he saw Sarah standing at the curb.

The Toyota's passenger-side door let out a loud creak as Sarah opened it and slid in.

"I saw you drive by, so I thought I'd come down and wait for you here. I know your car, it's rather unmistakable."

"It's a ride," Josh said, trying not to sound apologetic.

"You look different," he said, immediately regretting such a clumsy greeting. "I mean you look great. Never saw you with your hair down. Looks flattering. Really."

Sarah smiled and punched him lightly on the shoulder.

Sarah's new look was certainly different from how she presented herself at the station. Her bright red dress revealed curves Josh had never imagined before. Her hair hung softly along each cheek.

She had traded her wire-rim glasses for ones with large circular frames that enhanced the size and color of her brown eyes. And she was wearing lipstick, bright red to match her dress. Josh's eyes wandered down from her eyes and discovered a neckline that revealed, with more than a hint but less than a shout, the start of what promised to be a deep valley between two rounded hills. In a flash, Josh understood the reason for the hoodies at work.

They arrived at Gandalf's, a restaurant known for its extensive vegan menu. Josh had researched it on the internet.

He pulled the Toyota into the lot next door, hoping no one had seen them get out of the creaky beast.

Sarah took his arm, which surprised him, coming from a woman whose daily attire was the Western equivalent of a burka.

"Better than a punch on the shoulder," he thought.

The menu seemed to impress Sarah. She chose a Mediterranean-based entrée, while Josh followed suit with a vegetable curry.

"Good choice, this place," she said. "I've read about it. And by the way, you don't have to go all vegan on my account. You could've had a steak. I mean, if they had steak."

Josh felt his cheeks redden. "I'll remember that next time."

Again, he mentally kicked himself. How could he assume there would be a next time?

Josh saw a hint of a smile as she looked down at her plate. His eyes wandered downward to her neckline. She had leaned forward and revealed more of the path through that heretofore hidden valley. He looked up an instant before she did. The last thing he wanted her to say was, "My eyes are up here."

Sarah scanned the dessert menu and picked the trio of gluten-free cookies with carob chips. She offered one to Josh to accompany his espresso. She saw his grimace after he took a bite.

"Tastes like cardboard, right?" she asked.

"I'll be honest — yes."

"You'll get used to it."

Josh felt his cheeks redden as the thought of "getting used to it" flashed through his mind. Maybe there would be a next time.

When he looked up again, he saw that Sarah's gaze was focused on something behind him.

"Don't turn around," she whispered. "There's a guy at the table closest to the door. He's looking at me — at us — and I hope he doesn't come over here."

"Who is it?" he whispered back.

"Someone I used to know. I don't want to talk with him."

"An old boyfriend?" Josh felt a rush of adrenaline at the thought of a rival interrupting just when things with Sarah were going well.

"No, it never got that far," she said. "His name's Greg. I don't want to walk past him when we leave."

Josh finished his wine and signaled the server for the check. He paid in cash so they could quickly stand up and leave. He told the waiter to keep the change and slipped him an extra ten to let them exit through the kitchen.

The waiter frowned and whispered that the chef didn't want customers in his kitchen.

"Sounds like my grandmother," Josh said. "Tell him we're restaurant critics, and we have to stay incognito."

While the waiter tried to follow the logic of that story, Josh and Sarah were halfway to the kitchen. They walked quickly past stacks of plates and bundles of arugula and found the back door.

From behind them, they heard the chef nervously ask the waiter, "They liked the food, didn't they?"

Once outside, Sarah motioned Josh to follow her across the alley, where they crouched down behind a dumpster.

"He might come looking for us. Let's stay here a while," she said.

Just then, the man from the table came out of the alley that ran along the side of the restaurant and strode to the back door. He yanked at the knob but found it locked.

"That's Greg," Sarah whispered.

Josh nodded and pulled Sarah out of sight. They both peeked over the top of the dumpster. They saw Greg give up on the door and run past the back of the next business and dart around the corner toward the front street.

"I think we're safe now," Josh said. "But let's stay here a while to make sure he's gone."

The night was silent but for the clanging of pans in the restaurant kitchen.

Josh and Sarah left the safety of the dumpster and jogged down the alley to where the car was parked.

Once inside the Toyota, Josh could see that Sarah was trembling and holding her red pumps in one hand.

"I can't run in heels," she said.

"I'll take you home, but you have to give me the story on this Greg person."

"I'd rather not, but for you, I will."

"Spill it," he said.

"OK, don't hate me, but it all started with a dating app."

"Two years ago, I went on ShotintheDark, it's a dating app for gamers. I thought I could start at Level Two, since whoever I met would have at least one thing in common with me."

"I swiped left on about a dozen dudes before I came to this guy who sounded right. His name was Greg. He was a skateboarder, and he was in a band. Sounded perfect at first."

"At first," Josh repeated, bringing in his interviewer skills.

"We met at a coffee place on Fillmore. It was great. We discovered we had a lot in common. And he wasn't bad looking. He looked just like the pic he posted."

"Except for the eye patch and the parrot," Josh teased.

"Close," she replied. He had a tattoo of the Roadrunner on his left bicep, and he had two skateboards with him, one with a Roadrunner and the other with Yosemite Sam. He invited me to skateboard down the Lombard Street Hill with him."

"Sounds like a fun first date."

"When I said no, he asked me to go with him and watch him do it."

"And you did?"

"We took an Uber to the top of Lombard — which I remember paying for. I have to say that dude was really good. He went through those hairpin turns like it was a giant slalom. He made it all the way to the bottom — and right into the arms of two cops waiting there. Some Lombard Street resident must have called the cops because of the noise."

"So, a scofflaw, right?"

"Wait, it gets better. Worse, actually. I Ubered back to the coffee shop and gave the manager the skateboard. Told him a dude named Greg would be back for it in a day or so."

"What happened to Greg?"

"Spent the night in jail. Next day, he paid his fine and went home. I texted him to tell him where his other skateboard was. He called me back and asked me out for the next night. Private suite at a Giants Game."

"Livin' the high life," Josh said as he gunned the Toyota up a freeway ramp.

His father is some muckety-muck in real estate. Connected, you know."

"Got it," Josh said and thought to himself that he couldn't compete with that level of muckety-muckness.

"He said he'd pick me up at my place, but I said no, I'd meet him at the ballpark. Next to the Willie Mays statue."

"Good move," Josh said.

"He was waiting there for me when I got out of the Uber. I could tell by his eyes that he's already had a few. He whisked me through a V.I.P. gate and up the elevator to the suite. All very posh. Four or five other dudes were already there — members of his band — and they were pretty sloshed. Greg introduced me as his new girlfriend and 'a helluva skateboarder'."

"I let the skateboarder thing pass, but the girlfriend line — I was like, 'Whoa, cowboy.'"

"Obviously, he liked you," Josh teased.

She answered with a punch to Josh's shoulder.

"So," she continued, "Greg proceeded to catch up with his buds. He ordered four beers and downed two of them in, like, two minutes. Then, he said to me, 'chug-a-lug.'"

"I just smiled. Took a sip and tried to watch the game. When I turned back, Greg had finished the last beer and ordered two more."

"The next thing you know, a foul ball thudded against the glass at the front of the booth, and all the guys whooped and cheered and tossed beer all over the place."

"Greg moved closer and started getting handsy. I tried to be polite and pushed him away, but he got worse."

Josh felt the hair rise on the back of his neck.

"Finally, I gave him a good shove that knocked him onto the floor, which got his bandmates whooping and hollering again. I grabbed my purse and fled."

She shoved her red pumps under Josh's nose. "Luckily, I wasn't wearing these."

"Did you ever hear from him again?"

"He started texting and leaving voicemails day and night for about a week, then he gave up — until tonight. Maybe I'm paranoid, but ever since, I've had the feeling he's following me. When I get on the bus after work, I check to see he's not there, too."

Josh found a parking spot right in front of Sarah's apartment.

She turned toward him. The streetlamp cast a glow on her dark brown hair. Josh cleared his throat and leaned toward her.

Sarah turned away, grabbed her purse, and pulled out her phone.

"Oh my god, I have to take this. I'm sorry."

Josh took a deep breath to slow his pounding heart.

"It's tonight? I totally forgot," she whispered into the phone.

She pushed the car door open, and the Toyota responded with a vicious creak.

"I'm sorry, Josh, but something has come up," she said as she took off her shoes. "You're welcome to come up. It's 2-F."

Sarah hiked up her dress and, with two shoes in the other hand, sprinted up the walk and up the steps to her building.

Curiosity trumping frustration, Josh strode quickly after her.

The door to 2-F was ajar, and sounds of gunfire filled the hall. Josh slipped inside and flattened himself against the wall. In the dim light, he could see Sarah seated on the edge of a couch, wearing black virtual reality goggles. She held a controller between her knees while she manipulated the two joysticks.

"Sorry, but the Black Marauders have challenged us to a duel," she said. "I thought it was tomorrow night."

Josh had never seen her more engaged, not even in front of her computer screens at work.

"If we win this, we'll be in first place. Hey, Hendricks, watch your back, there's a starship coming up."

Josh waved his hand in front of her goggled face. She did not respond and began rapidly clicking the controller.

"Hendricks is our captain. He's in Johannesburg." More clicking. "I had a great time, really. But I'm committed to my team. You're welcome to stay, but this could take hours."

"That's OK. I understand commitment. See you tomorrow."

Josh took one last look at Sarah, barefoot, red dress, VR goggles, as he slipped out the door.

The next morning, Josh arrived at the radio station. He whisked by Sarah's office and went directly to his desk. The mixed signals he received from the previous night made him unsure of what to say to Sarah. The issue was forced an hour later when Sarah walked into his cubicle and set a mug of coffee on his desk.

"Here you go. No cream, no sugar."

Josh looked at her but stayed silent.

"It's a peace offering for last night," she said. "I didn't plan on getting so involved in the VR game."

Josh let her off the hook. "But you were committed. You couldn't let your team down."

Sarah stifled a yawn and said, "Yeah, my priorities suck, but you were smart not to stick around. We didn't finish until three a.m." She allowed herself a full yawn.

"How'd you do?"

"We lost. Now, we're in third place."

"Sorry."

"But I have good news for you. Sort of, anyway. Your half-sister's adoptive parents, Janet and Phillip Carter, moved from Kalamazoo three years ago. They live in Florida now. I'm going through Florida records."

She stifled another yawn.

"There sure are a lot more Larsons in Florida than I would have thought. But so far, not those two. The Florida DMV is stingy with its records. But I need a break before I get back on that. Besides, I have a job here, too."

"Yeah, I need to get back to mine. See you at lunch."

Later, Josh came into her office with two bags of Chinese takeout and his half-sister's graduation photo.

"Maybe we should focus on her photo. Could be a clue here," he said.

Sarah opened her bag.

"You forgot the soy sauce."

"Sorry," Josh grunted.

"No worries, I think I have some in my desk."

"You would, wouldn't you?"

"Smart ass," she said and punched him on the arm.

"What about the cap and gown?" he murmured through a mouthful of chow fun noodles. "The colors could tell us something."

The young woman wore a blue gown with a blue-and-gold sash and a gold tassel hanging from her mortarboard, contrasting with her dark red hair.

"Blue and gold," Sarah sighed. "I bet half the schools in the country fight for the blue and gold."

Sarah googled "college colors blue and gold."

The online search yielded more schools than Josh would have liked, UC Berkeley, UCLA, Florida International, Notre Dame, Southern, Toledo, Pitt, West Virginia, and Navy.

"We've got to narrow this down," he said.

Sarah squinted at the photo. "You can toss out Berkeley. We don't wear sashes."

"Navy, too. She isn't in uniform. Two down, seven to go." Josh jabbed his chopsticks into his chow fun.

Sarah pulled a magnifying glass from her desk and peered at the photo. "I'm not sure that color is gold," she whispered. It's too light for gold. More like yellow."

"It's an old photo," Josh said. It could have faded."

"But the blues are still blue. It's probably been kept out of the light for the last five years."

Josh tossed half of his egg roll into the bag. "I got an idea," he said, perhaps too loudly for office protocol.

"Shoot, dude."

Josh talked quickly. "I'll take the photo down to the lab and have them blow it up. Then, I'll take the blow-up to a paint store and have them analyze the color. That should show whether it's gold or yellow."

"I like it," she said.

Josh returned to his office, checked the newsfeed for breaking stories, and pounded out some copy for the afternoon news. Then, he searched the internet for the closest paint store that would still be open after six o'clock. The winner was Big Pagoda Paints on Fillmore.

The next morning, Josh dashed into Sarah's office with a list of colors.

"We just took a big step," he said. "The light color on her graduation outfit isn't gold, it's yellow, light yellow. The list of shades I got from the paint store was Morning Buttercup, Baby Canary, Buttered Buns, and Amazing Maize."

"Baby Canary, how cute," she said sarcastically.

He ignored her gibe. "No, I went through that list of colleges online, and it has to be maize. Maize and Blue. There are only two schools on that list whose colors are maize and blue – the University of Michigan and a little school in Minnesota." He looked down at his list again. "It's called, let's see, Carleton.

"Never heard of it."

"Me neither. But it's got to be Michigan. She grew up in Michigan."

Sarah let out a slow sigh. "You realize that there are, like, fifty thousand students at Michigan."

"We'll find her. We just have to contact the alumni department."

"I guess we'd better get started," she said and turned back to her computer screen.

Josh looked at his watch. "Crap, I'm on the air in five minutes. We'll have to pick this up after the noon break."

Sarah went online and found the number for the University of Michigan Student Records department. Josh made the call and was placed on hold by the robotic voice at the other end.

"Damn artificial intelligence," he muttered.

They spent the next several minutes listening to a tinny recording of Ode to Joy, until Josh hung up in frustration.

"Hey," Sarah said, "now you've lost your place in the queue."

"That's enough joy for me, let's call the other school. The one in Minnesota."

Sarah found the number for the Carleton College student records department, and Josh punched the numbers into his cell phone.

The voice at the other end was human and sounded cheerful.

"Student records, this is Olga."

Josh explained that he was trying to reach his adopted sister, whom he had never met, and he needed a way to contact her.

"We suspect that she graduated from Carleton somewhere between 2015 and 2018 and that her last name was Larson."

Olga responded with a standard answer — the college didn't provide such personal information about their students.

Sarah whispered to Josh that she'd heard this answer a thousand times and told him to sound more desperate.

Josh nodded and jumped into the story of how his aging grandparents were searching for the granddaughter whom their daughter had given birth to — a baby girl who was tragically given up for adoption. And how, later, this granddaughter died, leaving them with a newborn grandson who was now desperate to find his sister and gain some small connection, through his sister, to his deceased mother and bring closure for his beloved grandparents.

Josh thought he heard Olga let out a sob.

"Oh, Sweetie, that's so sad. What is your sister's name?"

"All I know is that she was adopted by a couple named Larson."

"Oh, my goodness, can you imagine the number of Larsons who come to this school every year? We're in Minnesota, doncha know? But, let me try a search."

Olga put him on hold, and Josh and Sarah exchanged a high five.

When Olga came back, she asked, "Is that Larson with an O or an E?"

"I'm pretty sure it's an O, Josh answered. "I have a photo of her in her graduation robes. She has red hair and was wearing a walking boot."

Olga brightened. "Oh, you're looking for Krissy Larson. Everyone here remembers her. She was a soccer star and led us to the D-3 National Championship. She's wearing that boot because she broke her ankle scoring the winning goal against St. Olaf. Poor girl had to limp across the stage to get her diploma. She turned pro, and she's doin' real well."

Olga's voice went fuzzy as she called to someone else in the office.

"Hey, Louann, what's the team Krissy Larson plays for? The soccer team?"

Olga came back with the answer. "She plays for the Baltimore Barbies. You could Google her."

Josh and Sarah filled the air with fist-pumps.

Josh thanked Olga for her help, and Sarah jumped back onto her computer.

"Baltimore Barbies, here you go."

Josh leaned over Sarah's shoulder, and their cheeks touched.

She scrolled down the list of team members until — and there she was — "Krissy Larson, Striker, WSL First Team All Star 2020, 2021, Highest Total Goals, 2020, 2021." But, not mentioned was the detail that meant more to Josh than anything else — she was his mother's child and his half-sister. And there was her photo. Even at postage-stamp size, her red hair was unmistakable.

Further down the page was a paragraph about the Baltimore Barbies: "Established 1999, President and CEO, Franz Guttmann.

Owned by Tomashita Toys, a Division of WorldCo Group Enterprises, Ltd. Team name "The Barbies" derived from Tamashita Toys' signature product, the Barbie Doll."

"So, your sister's a Barbie," giggled Sarah. "I guess that makes you a Ken."

"No, it makes me happy. Ecstatic. Over the moon."

He put his arms around Sarah and hugged her tightly.

"And I've got you to thank for it."

Josh took a deep breath and dialed the main office of the Baltimore Barbies. Sarah grabbed his hand and held tight.

A recorded voice gave detailed instructions for purchasing Barbies' tickets, followed by a listing of the team's home games for the rest of the season.

Josh drummed his fingers on the desk.

Finally, the voice said to stay on the line if you want to speak with an operator.

Sarah slapped Josh's hand to stop the drumming.

"Baltimore Barbies. What do you want?" said a human voice.

Josh explained that he wanted to speak with Krissy Larson because she was his long-lost half-sister.

"Well, that's a new one," the voice answered. "Look, if you want free tickets, tell your story to PR, maybe they'll give you half a ticket."

The voice snorted out a laugh but went on. "Leave your name and number, and if she wants to call you back, she will."

Josh spelled out his name and slowly recited his number.

"Don't hold your breath, half-bro," the voice said, snorted again, and hung up.

"I bet she calls," Sarah said.

"Hope so," he sighed.

That night, Josh lay awake wondering if Krissy would call.

"I could try calling again, but how long should I wait? Have to be careful she doesn't think I'm stalking her."

His phone pinged with a text, and he grabbed for the nightstand. His phone said three AM.

It was Sarah.

"U up? Hear anything? She's three hours ahead of us," she texted.

"Thanks for the tip on time zones," he texted back. Yes, I'm up, and no, she hasn't called."

"Don't be fussy. I'm as nervous as you are."

"Sorry."

"That's OK. We should hear something tomorrow. If your message got passed on to her."

"Now I've got THAT to worry about."

"Oops, sorry. I'm no help."

"Yes, you are. I'll go get a glass of wine."

"Good idea. G'night."

The next morning, Josh leaned into Sarah's office and held up two pairs of crossed fingers. Sarah gave him a thumbs-up.

They went down the street to a Thai restaurant for lunch.

They had just ordered when Josh's phone buzzed. He wrenched the phone out of his pocket and fumbled to answer.

It was Krissy Larson.

"I'm looking for the guy who says he's my half-brother."

The waitress came by, and Sarah waved her away.

"That's me. I'm Josh Tanner. We've been trying to contact you. I'm calling from San Francisco."

Josh took a deep breath. "We share the same birth mother."

Silence at the other end.

"Look, Krissy, I'm sure you're my half-sister. You were adopted in Oregon by Janet and Phillip Larson. You graduated from —"

Josh suddenly drew a blank.

"From Carleton College," Sarah whispered loudly.

"From Carleton College in Minnesota. You were on the soccer team, a star, and you broke your ankle in your final game. You grew up in Kalamazoo, and your parents moved to Florida two years ago."

"What did you do, hack into the DMV?" Krissy asked.

Josh decided to play his trump card. "When you were adopted, you were wearing a bracelet with a topaz ring attached to it."

Krissy gasped, "Oh, my god, I want to meet you."

Josh summarized their common past — their grandparents in El Cerrito and their mother, who died when he was born. He was solemn when he mentioned her father, a student athlete who had red hair. He left out any mention of his own father, figuring that could come later — if at all.

Through her tears, Krissy said she would be on the West Coast the following week when The Barbies played the Santa Clara Microchips.

Josh suggested they meet at a restaurant near the stadium in Santa Clara, and he would text her the address.

"I can't wait to meet you," she said, "But I'm elated and scared all at the same time."

"Same here, Sis, same here," he said.

Josh and Sarah were sitting at a window table at a popular Greek eatery called Opa-Opa, waiting to meet Krissy. The day before, Sarah suggested his sister would be more at ease not meeting Josh for the first time in a dark corner of a nearly deserted restaurant.

"It's like the first meeting you get from an online dating app," she told him. "They always tell you to meet at a public place with a lot of people around. Safer to meet a stranger that way."

"Even if it turns out to be a skateboarder named Brad?"

"It was Greg, and don't be a shit." Sarah punched him on the arm, this time so hard he flinched and let out a gasp.

Two tall women walked by the window and turned into the restaurant. They stopped inside the door, and the one with the curly red hair looked in their direction. It had to be Krissy.

Josh waved, and the redhead started over to the table, followed by her companion, a slim woman with her hair tucked into a Baltimore Ravens cap.

"She's brought a friend, just to be safe," Sarah whispered.

"Stop it," Josh hissed through clenched teeth.

Josh stood up, and Krissy grabbed him into a hug and held him tightly. Sarah and the other woman smiled at each other.

Krissy let go of Josh and both were in tears.

"I know it's you, I just know it," she said.

"Looks right to me," her friend said.

The four of them sat down opposite each other, and Krissy introduced her companion.

"This is Tommie — Thomasina Klinski — she's our all-star goalie and my very best friend." Krissy reached over and squeezed Tommy's hand.

Josh hugged Sarah. "This is my BFF, Sarah Coughlin. Without her, I never would have found you."

Sarah wondered if Best Friend Forever would be the pinnacle of their growing relationship.

The conversation continued through alternating laughter and tears. Krissy asked Josh where he had gone to college, and he explained his six-year trek through San Francisco State.

"I was lucky to graduate in four years, thanks to my mystery benefactor. My parents couldn't have afforded Carleton."

"We love mysteries," Sarah said. "Do tell."

Krissy explained that after she had been accepted at the school, she received a letter from the Williamson Foundation, along with a check for her first year's tuition. An accompanying letter stated that if she sent copies of her semester grades each year, along with a photo of herself, her tuition would be paid for the following year.

Krissy leaned across the table to Josh.

"Now, I want to know how you got my graduation picture."

Josh felt his mouth and throat go dry.

"Where was this letter from? Who signed it?" he croaked.

"They were never signed personally, just 'Cordially, The Williamson Foundation'. And every year, they came from a P.O. box in Houston. At first, my parents thought it was a joke, but the checks always cleared. I sent thank-you letters along with my grades, but I never heard from them. Only the checks."

"Pretty amazing, right?" Tommie said.

Josh looked at Sarah as he spoke. "I think those checks came from my father. Fred Williamson. He lived in Houston, and I visited him before he died. He gave me the photo and said, 'You have a sister.'"

Krissy let out a gasp. "Fred Williamson! Fred Williamson was a friend of my parents when we lived in Houston. He must have known who I was, but he never let on."

"He tracked you back to the orphanage through your parents," Sarah said. "Reverse engineering."

Krissy sat motionless, as if she were hypnotized.

Sarah turned to Josh. "He never paid your tuition, did he?" she asked.

"Are you kidding?" Josh snorted, "He sent me a check for one hundred dollars every birthday — or birth month — I don't think he knew what day I was born."

Josh shook his head before continuing. "One hundred dollars

and always with the same note, 'Stay strong, don't go soft.'"

Krissy reached over and grabbed his hand. "I'm devastated that he treated you so coldly when he was treating me well — money-wise, I mean," she said.

"No, don't beat yourself up," Tommy said. "Josh was his son, and you were his stepdaughter. He gave you money because you're a girl. Girls need a leg up. Josh got nothing because the Old Man knew that dudes have the advantages in this world as long as they stay strong and don't — what was it?"

"Don't go soft," Josh answered.

"Tommy, do you think I'm soft?" Krissy asked.

"Hell, no, not the way you kick ass out on the pitch."

The three women laughed, but Josh stared silently into his drink. Finally, he looked up and said, "Well, I guess the Old Man did us both a favor. I'm happy for you, Sis."

They had been drinking ouzo, and Sarah proposed a toast.

"Here's to an amazing reunion and a happy ending for all of us."

The four of them exchanged hugs like it was New Year's Eve.

Krissy invited them to come to the next afternoon's game against the Microchips. Josh proposed that he and Sarah take Krissy and Tommy to meet their grandparents in El Cerrito after the game.

"Hey, great," Sarah said. "They get to ride in your car."

Josh punched her on the arm.

Josh and Sarah fell silent as he drove her home. She leaned her head on his shoulder.

"I owe you everything. I never would have found her without you," he said.

"I'm happy for you," she said as she snuggled closer.

When they parked in front of her apartment, Josh turned and kissed her. They lingered for a long minute before she pulled away.

"Come on in. There's something I want to show you," she whispered.

Josh followed her inside, and she waved toward the couch.

"Have a seat, and I'll bring it out."

Josh sat on the couch. Sarah called from the bedroom.

"You can turn on the Xbox. It's set for Road Warrior Two."

"Do you have Pac-Man?" he said.

"LOL," she yelled back.

A few minutes later, she appeared in the bedroom doorway. Josh blinked and squinted at her.

Sarah was wrapped in a red-and-blue star-spangled cape. She had let her hair down, and on her head was a gold tiara with a red star on the front. A pair of red boots showed from beneath the bottom of the cape.

"You called me Wonder Woman once, so here she is."

After Josh found his voice, he stammered, "Well, I meant it. I still mean it."

"Thanks, Josh."

"What did Wonder Woman call her cape?"

"This is my Cape of Invisibility," said Sarah, as she spread the cape open.

"Now, you see me."

Josh felt his heart race. Sarah was wearing red knee-high boots, a tiara, and nothing else.

Just as suddenly, she drew the cape in around her.

"And now, you don't," she giggled.

Josh nodded slowly. "You're a wonder, all right. But not that good at invisibility."

He strode quickly toward her, and as the romance novels would say, gathered her in his arms as she pressed her lips against his.

"Lose the boots," he whispered. "But keep the tiara."

Josh woke up with sunlight streaming through Sarah's bedroom window. Sarah rolled over to him and planted a kiss on his forehead.

"That was nice," she said as she ran her fingers down his cheek.

"I think I love you," he said.

"Only 'think'? Because I know I love you."

"Let me rephrase that," he said and pulled her closer, "I am one-hundred percent sure I love you."

"It wasn't just the costume, then?"

"Well, maybe a little," he grinned.

Sarah growled and began to tickle him until he begged her to stop.

"OK, OK, it wasn't the costume. He pulled her to him and whispered, "It was the real Wonder Woman inside."

Sarah propped herself up on one elbow as a wave of seriousness washed over her face.

"I have a confession to make," she said.

Josh took a quick breath and held it.

"The night you took me home and I said I had to take a call — well, there was no call. I made it all up."

"But the video game you said you lost…"

"There wasn't a game, not that night. It really was the next night. I was pretending. I mean, I wasn't ready, or I didn't think I was ready to get more involved with you. I was scared I'd screw things up."

"Those goggles weren't a turn-off, if that's what you were hoping."

Sarah let the comment pass.

"But I've had time to think it over, and now I know I want to be with you. I have since you used that lame 'asking for a friend' excuse. You're a terrible liar, and I love you for it."

They melted together in a long embrace.

As Josh's hand slid up her thigh, she sat up.

"Now who's ticklish?" he asked.

"No, look at the clock. It's noon and the match starts at two."

They jumped out of bed and scrambled for their clothes.

"You wearing the tiara?"

"No, stupid, that was just for you."

"I am honored," he said, still looking for his left shoe.

Krissy had wrangled excellent seats for the game: midfield, right behind the Barbies' bench. The match bounced back and forth, as the Microchips were able to fend off the Barbies' aggressive style.

Josh was mesmerized seeing his sister sprint up and down the field, her long red hair flying out behind her. He wondered what life would have been like if they'd grown up together.

Krissy's adept ball-handling allowed her to score both the Barbies' goals. He had read about her on the Barbies' website and realized she deserved her nickname — "The Red Menace."

Near the end, a defensive lapse enabled the Microchips to respond with a goal of their own. The Barbies' lead was cut in half, now at 2 to 1. The Microchips' fans came alive with cheers and foot-stomping. Someone in the crowd blared a vuvuzela.

With only seconds to play, a Microchip midfielder stole an errant pass and headed straight for the Barbies' goal.

Josh was hoarse from cheering and was only able to mouth the words, "Stop her, she's going to score."

Maybe it was ESP or the special bond between siblings, but Krissy appeared out of nowhere and stopped the would-be scorer with a slide that cut the Microchip player's legs out from under her.

"That's not good," Sarah whispered in resignation. She looked at Josh biting his thumb in frustration. She pulled his hand away and squeezed it.

Good and bad. Krissy thwarted the Microchip's last-second chance to end the match in a tie. But her aggressive tackle gave the fallen Microchip the opportunity to grab her own leg and howl in pain.

"Crap, she's faking," Josh muttered. "She flopped like a Frenchman."

Fake injury or not, the referee flashed a red card at Krissy and tossed her out of the match. The hometown crowd went wild with anger as the target of Krissy's tackle was helped off the field.

Krissy walked back to the Barbies' bench and looked up at Josh. Her right eye was swollen and on its way to black and blue.

Josh raised both arms in a "what happened?" gesture and pointed to his own eye.

Krissy slapped her elbow, pointed to her eye, and gestured toward the Microchip bench.

"Had to be deliberate," Sarah shouted. "I hope she's OK."

"Probably not the first time," Josh said.

The Microchips hastened to assemble in front of the Barbies' goal, ready for the penalty kick. With only seconds remaining, a successful penalty kick would end the match in a 2-2 tie.

Tommie, the Barbies' goalie, sidled back and forth at the mouth of the goal. The tallest of the Microchips, a dark-haired girl well over six feet in height, took her time placing the ball for the penalty kick. She stepped back, then moved forward to reposition the ball barely an inch to the left. It was a ploy to rattle Tommie, who was hunched over, ready to spring. A breeze swept across the pitch and caused the net to billow to the right. Tommie rocked back and forth on the balls of her feet.

Josh hugged Sarah around her shoulders. "She's going to Tommie's right, lower corner," he rasped. "Come on, Tommie."

"I can't look," Sarah whispered. Josh's hug, added to the tenseness on the field, sent her heart racing.

Krissy stood on the sideline with fists clenched. "You got this, Tommie," she shouted into the breeze.

The Microchip jogged toward the ball. The silence of the crowd was broken by the thud of a boot on leather, and the ball twisted high towards the left corner.

Josh had guessed wrong about the direction of the kick. But Tommie had not. She dove high to her right, arms outstretched. The ball struck Tommie square in the face and bounced clear of the goal. Her instincts preserved the Barbies' 2-1 win. The crowd groaned, Josh and Sarah jumped into the air and exchanged kisses, and Krissy ran onto the field and wrapped Tommie in a victory hug. The rest of the Barbies ran in all directions, screaming and pumping their fists.

Krissy looked down at her jersey and saw it was covered in blood. Tommie was bleeding from her nose and mouth.

"I think they broke my nose," Tommie said, wiping her face on her sleeve.

The stadium parking lot was now nearly empty. The Barbies' team bus had already left for their hotel, but without Krissy and Tommie. Josh and Sarah leaned against the Toyota, waiting for the two remaining Barbies to join them.

The door of the players' entrance opened, and Krissy and Tommie walked out. When they got to the car, Tommie sported two black eyes and a wide white bandage taped across her nose. Krissy's right eye was now a real shiner.

"Great game, you were spectacular," Josh said. "But, if you don't feel like you can make it to Grandma's, they will understand."

"No, they won't," Krissy shot back. "You found their granddaughter for them, and we've got to show up. I'm dying to meet them,

"Me, too," Tommie said.

"What about your nose and your eye?" Sarah asked.

"Not the first time I've broken it. It'll heal. Sorry, I look like a raccoon."

"I feel like a cyclops. And it was my bad. My red card caused this whole mess."

"It was a clean tackle," Josh said. You were robbed."

Krissy hugged him. "Thanks, bro, I already love you so much."

It was a long drive through traffic to get to Ben and Lois's in El Cerrito. Being the shortest, Sarah had volunteered to sit in the back of the Toyota. Tommie joined her, telling Krissy to sit up front with her brother.

"You two have been apart forever. You need to sit together," Tommie said. She settled back in the seat and promptly fell asleep.

Josh knew his grandmother would have dinner prepared, so he warned them about the canned pear half suspended in lime jello and topped with a dollop of Miracle Whip.

Questions flew back and forth: where did they live, what were their jobs, how often did their team practice, what were their college majors, and was anyone into gaming? The conversation moved to what they wanted for the future. Sarah said "gaming design," Josh wanted to produce documentaries, and Krissy said law school after soccer. But first, she wanted to play in Europe.

Without opening her eyes, Tommie said, "South America. They are more passionate than Europeans. And I want to live in Buenos Aires."

"No, Brazil is where the real passion is," Sarah piped up.

"Actually, we'll go wherever we get the best offer," said Krissy. "And, Josh, you can document our rise to the top."

"I'll design an immersive VR program that provides the total soccer experience, and Krissy and Tommie will be the stars."

Josh found it hard to tell whether Sarah was serious or joking. Her idea ran through his mind until Krissy interrupted with a question out of the blue.

"Josh, do you know who my father was?"

His brain whirled to catch another train of thoughts — how would he tell her? How would he start?

"I do," he said. "But…"

"But, what?" There was an edge to her voice that he had never heard before. He felt like she was playing the Big Sister card, and he wondered what their life might have been like if they had grown up together.

He blurted out the answer. "He died a long time ago."

Josh recounted what he and Sarah had learned about Krissy's father, the red-haired quarterback killed in a motorcycle crash.

Krissy sat back in her seat and remained quiet for the rest of the drive.

When the four of them pulled into the driveway, Josh's grandparents were waiting on the porch. Lois ran to the car before anyone could get out, while Ben followed slowly, nervously, preparing himself for the shock of meeting his granddaughter.

Lois singled out her daughter's red-haired child, locked her in a maternal embrace, and wouldn't let go. Ben stood frozen before he joined Lois in an all-enveloping hug. Tears dripped from six pairs of eyes like icicles melting in a spring thaw.

After the hug relaxed, Krissy took Tommie's hand and, through her sobs, announced,

"This is Tommie, my best friend."

She pointed to Josh and declared, "This is my new brother who found me for you."

"And this is Sarah, whom I've told you about," Josh said, squeezing her to him.

Lois let go of Krissy and transferred her hug to Sarah.

"You are more beautiful than I imagined," she said, and blotted her eyes with a tissue that always appears magically in a grandmother's hand.

"Krissy, how did you get that shiner?" Ben asked. "And, Tommie, what about your nose?"

"Tommie blocked a shot with her face," said Krissy. "And I took an elbow to the eye."

"Soccer gets rough sometimes," said Tommie.

Ben's chest swelled with indignation. "Did you get a penalty kick out of it?"

"Ben, we can talk sports inside. Come on, everyone, dinner is just about ready. I hope you all like pot roast."

Josh started to say that Sarah was a vegan, but she gave him an elbow to the ribs.

"I'll be fine," she hissed. "I don't want to get a black mark in your grandmother's book."

Ben directed the seating around the table — Josh and Sarah on one side, Krissy and Tommie on the other, with Ben and Lois at either end. Lois could be heard in the kitchen clanking some utensil against a pot.

"Can we help you?" Sarah called out.

"No, I'm fine. It'll be ready in a minute," Lois replied.

Ben sighed, "That's Lois's way of saying 'stay out of my kitchen.' You'll learn."

"I'll learn," Sarah thought as she felt a wave of excitement flow over her. She hoped those two words signaled Ben's acceptance of her. Now, she was further motivated to toss aside her vegan rules and eat the pot roast.

Josh pointed to the green, pear-infused Jello sitting to the side of each plate.

"See, that's the jello salad I told you about," he explained to the girls.

"I love jello!" Krissy exclaimed.

From across the table, Sarah flashed her a thumbs-up.

The mood at dinner was joyous. Lois and Ben peppered Krissy with questions about her life over the past decades while Tommie ate with relish, and Sarah fought her way through the slice of pot roast.

Before dessert, Ben brought out a box of photographs highlighting the life of Krissy's mother. Lois, Krissy, and Sarah sobbed. Tommie and Ben blotted their eyes with their napkins. Even though Josh had seen them many times before, he teared up as well. He fetched a box of tissues from the sideboard and set it in the middle of the table.

They came to a photo of Jeanette at her sixteenth birthday party. She was smiling as she extended her hand to display her gift — the topaz ring.

Lois wiped her eyes again and fixed her eyes on Krissy.

"Sweetheart, do you have that topaz ring? Jeanette threaded it on a shoelace and hung it around your wrist before…" She broke into sobs. "Before she gave you up? It was the last thing she did for you."

Krissy looked at Tommie before replying. Her throat was tight.

"Well, in a way, yes," she answered.

"In a way? What do you mean?" Lois asked.

"Tommie wears it now," Krissy replied.

Tommie leaned forward and stretched her left hand toward Lois. On her third finger, glowing in the light from the dining room chandelier, was the topaz ring.

"Tommie and I are a couple; we're married," Krissy said.

Sarah poked Josh with an elbow.

"Told you," she whispered.

Krissy held her left hand out to Lois. "And this is the ring Tommie gave to me."

Krissy wore a gold ring set with a round ruby.

"It was my mother's," Tommie said.

The room went silent. Josh's gaze alternated between his grandmother's face and the framed photo of his mother on the mantle.

"Good for you — both of you," Lois said. "No better way to keep your rings in the family."

"I agree," Ben said. "Now, we have two granddaughters."

He looked over at Sarah and added, "Maybe three."

Sarah lowered her head, but Josh could see she was blushing.

"Well, time for dessert," Lois announced and trotted off to the kitchen.

It was dark when the newly united four drove back to the hotel where the Barbies were staying. The team would fly out in the morning for their match in Phoenix. Krissy and Tommie were asleep in the back seat, thanks to the extra-strength Tylenol Ben had given them for their injuries.

The Barbies' hotel was less than first class. The Mont d'Or was a motel with exterior corridors and ice machines at the base of each stairwell. As she got out of the car, Tommie called it "the typical Barbie dump."

"You always stay in places like this?" Josh asked.

"This is one of the better ones," Tommie said. "Hopefully, there won't be any drug deals going down outside our window."

The four of them exchanged hugs. Krissy told Josh she would call him when they got to Phoenix.

"The season ends in a month," Krissy said. "We'll fly out from Baltimore, so we can spend some quality time with you and exchange family histories."

"Great, you can stay with us," Sarah said.

After a last round of hugs, Krissy and Tommie trudged over to the Mont d'Or.

"Stay with us,'" Josh thought. "I like the sound of that."

On the way back to San Francisco, Josh and Sarah remained lost in their thoughts until he broke the silence.

"A lot of news to lay on Ben and Lois. Right, babe?"

"Breaking news, sweetie, breaking news. That's what you do best." Sarah replied.

EPILOGUE

Josh's place was larger and closer to downtown, so Sarah gave up her apartment and moved in with him. She brought her window box sprouting basil and thyme, and they acquired a cat, a female

Russian Blue they named Ludmilla.

Sarah was pouring Saturday morning tea when Josh came in with the mail they had forgotten to retrieve from the box the day before.

"Anything good?" Sarah asked.

"Could be bad," he said. "A letter from a law firm. Maybe we're being sued."

The return address on the tan envelope said, "Jurndice and Jurndice, Attorneys at Law, Houston, Texas." Josh grabbed a table knife and slit it open. When he pulled out the single-page letter, a smaller slip of paper fell out and fluttered to the floor. Josh started to read, silently, only moving his lips.

"OK, what's it say?" Sarah asked.

"It's addressed to me. 'Dear Mr. Tanner, The estate of your father, Frederick James Williamson, has been settled, and as executor, Jurndice and Jurndice, LLC., is authorized to send you the enclosed check as your portion of said estate. An equal amount will be available to your half-sister, Kristina Louise Larson (address unknown) at such time as she contacts us. If you are able to reach Ms. Larson, please ask her to contact us at the address below.

In accordance with the wishes of your father, the Houston house and all of its contents, and the 1999 Jaguar XKE are passed on to Ms. Elise M. Crandall. If you have any questions, please contact us at the address below. Sincerely, Travis B. Jurndice, Attorney at Law.'"

Josh sat down so heavily that tea spilled from both cups. Sarah had picked up the slip of paper and was staring at it.

"What is it?" Josh asked.

"The check," she said and thrust it towards him.

Josh accepted the check from her, took a breath, and read it.

"Six hundred eighty thousand, nine hundred and forty dollars and fifty cents."

Both gulped down what was left of their tea.

"There's a letter, too. From Houston. Better check it out," she said.

Josh tore open the envelope and pulled out a typed single-spaced letter wrapped around a sheet of lined yellow paper with writing in blue ink. He looked at Sarah as if for permission to start reading.

"It's from Elise, my father's caregiver," he said and began with the handwritten note. 'Dear Josh, this letter was dictated to me by your father shortly before he went into the hospital, where you visited him. It was his wish that I say nothing to you about it while you were here, since he wanted it sent after his passing and the estate was settled. I assume you have heard from his attorneys. With my own best wishes, Elise Crandall'"

Josh stared at the typed letter.

"Read it, please read it," Sarah whispered.

Josh smoothed the papers and began.

"Dear Josh, since I am almost at the end of the road, I want to clarify some issues that have been weighing on me for many years.

First of all, I really did love your mother, still do, and not a day goes by that I don't think of her. I was away on a university-sponsored exploration trip to Venezuela when she sent me a message that she was pregnant.

I left for the States as soon as I could to be with her. When I arrived, I found that she had suffered some sort of psychological trauma. She was staying with her parents, who refused to let me see her. I should add that her father stood at the front door with a shotgun, which I assumed was loaded.

Early in our relationship, she had confided to me that several years earlier, she had given birth to a child whom she had given up for adoption. That would have been your half-sister."

At this point, Elise had entered her own note.

"Your father's mind wandered, and I was confused about what he said next, but I'll pick up where he got back on track. — Elise."

"I hope Elise didn't miss too much," Josh said.

"Keep reading," Sarah said impatiently.

Josh continued, "I quickly wrapped up my teaching duties and planned to stick around Berkeley, in hopes that your mother would come back to herself, and I would be able to get back into her life. But in her eighth month, she hemorrhaged and was rushed to the hospital. You know the rest — you were born, and she died. I tried to see her, but your grandparents wouldn't let me. I took the coward's way out and returned to Venezuela. I couldn't face what my life would be like in California. I joined a Houston-based oil exploration company and cut all ties with the university. My twenty-three years in South America were very successful, money-wise, but wreaked havoc with my health. I returned to Houston and retired on my earnings.

I hired a detective who had connections with the FBI, and through him, I was able to track down your sister living with her adoptive parents in Michigan."

"Geez, if only we'd had the money for a detective," Sarah said.

"Hey, you're the only detective we need. You did great," Josh said.

"Thanks, Babe," Sarah said and Josh continued reading, "To find a small measure of penance in being the primal cause of your mother's death, I paid Krissy's college costs for four years, but I lost track of her and her parents after she graduated from Carleton, so I will leave that task to you.

Josh, I was not so generous with you. Your reward will be granted to you after my death. I have withheld it because I wanted you to fight for what you earn in life. As I said to you in the past, I don't want you to go soft, but to stay strong. I know your mother, the fighter that she was, would agree.

When you visit the house, you will see a collection of my paintings. They are my attempts to honor the memory of your mother. She is the woman who appears in each of the paintings. I have left instructions to have one of these paintings shipped to you as a link to our shared past. May you be blessed with success, Dad."

Josh dropped the letter on the table and shook his head as he searched for his voice. "This is crazy. Just crazy," he said.

"No," Sarah replied. "This is what he wanted."

"And he signed it 'Dad'. Not 'Frederick G. Williamson,' like all the other times. It's like a deathbed conversion," Josh said.

"And now, you've won the jackpot," she said.

"No, Sweetie, we've hit the jackpot."

"You can change jobs, do what you want. There's nothing more for you at the station," she said.

"My head is spinning. The money, the painting. I just hope it's not the one I'm thinking of."

Sarah wrinkled her brows in puzzlement. "Why not? What's wrong?"

Josh grabbed Sarah and held her tightly for a long minute.

"I've never needed you more," he whispered.

When he finally let go of her, he reached for his phone.

"I can't concentrate right now," he said. "I've got to call Krissy. Where is she now?"

"Florida. They're playing in Orlando tomorrow."

Josh dialed Krissy's cell number and turned to Sarah.

"What should we do now?" he asked.

"I think we can quit our day jobs."

THE ONGOING LIFE OF MARGO MACOMBER

(With a salute to Ernest Hemingway)

"It is the ruling of this court that the death of Francis Macomber was accidental, and that no guilt shall be assigned. Therefore, Mrs. Macomber, you are free to go. The court extends its condolences for your loss."

Margo Macomber looked over at Robert Wilson as he let out a short puff of breath. They had been waiting in the sweltering Nairobi courtroom for two hours for the judge to appear with his verdict.

"However, Mr. Wilson, the court finds you negligent in the oversight of the use of firearms on your expedition and fines you the sum of one hundred pounds. You may pay your fine at the clerk's office outside."

Without a further word or glance at the former defendants, the judge turned and retraced his steps to his chambers.

Margo and Wilson walked back to her hotel through the Kenyan heat. They didn't speak until they were under the electric fan rotating lazily above their banquette at the hotel bar, gin gimlets in front of them.

"Sorry about the fine," she said.

Wilson took a sip of his gimlet and put it down, "Cost of doing business."

"Have you had incidents like this before?" She paused as she chose the word "incidents" intentionally.

"Rather not discuss it." He took another sip.

"Sorry. What do you do now?"

"Back to the Mathaiga Club. It's where all the guides stay. I have another tour coming up in a fortnight. Have to get back to nip any gossip in the bud."

"Gossip? About what?"

"The accident. Have to quell rumors before any of the chaps think about poaching my next client."

She stirred the nearly melted ice in her drink. "Any other gossip? About you and me?

"About bedding a client with her husband in the next tent? Let them think what they will," he said. She caught a twinkle in his eyes. "I've got a reputation to consider."

"As a ladies' man?"

"Mainly as a great white hunter."

Margo tugged at a lock of her hair, then brushed it back, "Maybe you could come up to my room. We'll see if we can spark a campfire."

She had spent the previous afternoon at the hotel salon getting a facial. "Those damned lines are starting to return," she whispered to herself. "Damn safari, damn Africa!" she shouted to the mirror.

Robert sat up and clenched his fist around his glass. A dark cloud passed over his eyes. "No more games. We shouldn't be seen together. No need for the Nairobi police to have second thoughts about the case." He leaned toward her and whispered, "Like a motive for the shooting."

"You are horrid," she said.

"No, I'm realistic. It's for your safety, too."

"Cold comfort," she replied. "I'm not used to being in such fraught circumstances. Also not used to being turned down. But I understand."

Robert took a deep breath and tried a lighter turn. "So, what's next for you?

"The coroner released the body to the mortuary. It will be ready tomorrow, and I'm having it delivered to the airport. My journey – Francis's and my journey – back to Connecticut begins tomorrow evening with a flight to Cairo. I'm taking Francis back to his mother."

"Then, I wish you godspeed." Robert stood up, laid some pound notes on the table, and walked out the door.

Margo watched him leave, swirling the remains of her gimlet. She knew it would have been simpler to have Francis cremated, much easier to transport him back to Connecticut. But she knew his mother would never forgive her if she missed the opportunity to see her darling boy one last time. Margo would not dare cross the old matriarch on this. "Grounds for being disowned," she muttered and lit a cigarette.

Besides the travel casket they put her husband in, Margo was taking back the lion skin, head and all, from the beast that made Francis turn tail and run. In her cable explaining Francis's demise to her mother-in-law, she said he had shot the lion himself. A not-so-little white lie to help Margo preserve her relationship with the old lady. No need to share her disgust at her husband's cowardice, at least not yet. Robert Wilson shot the lion. Or perhaps one of the gun bearers. The two men fired simultaneously as Francis fled past them.

But the trophy not going home was the head of the water buffalo on the next day's shoot. "Francis wanted to redeem himself for the lion business, poor fool," Margo thought.

The next day, they all went out for water buffalo, Robert Wilson leading the way through tall grass, followed by the bearer and Francis. Wilson demanded that Margo stay in the Land Rover, but she would have none of it.

"A buffalo is more dangerous than a lion, harder to bring down," Wilson said as he reluctantly handed her the loaded 6.5 Mannlicher.

"I can handle myself," she said. "It's Francis you should worry about."

Margo learned to shoot on a hunting trip to Colorado. She brought down two elk to Francis's one.

"Beginner's luck," she told him.

That night at the Colorado lodge, the guests in the next room banged on the wall in an attempt to quiet the couple. Everyone considered Margo a catch, a beauty whose face and figure graced the covers of numerous fashion magazines. But Francis matched her looks with his own: tall, slender, dark eyes and hair, a more-than-mortal sight on the tennis courts and polo fields. Exeter, Yale, and sailing around the Bahamas. And of course, the money. His father built an insurance and real estate empire beginning in Hartford and spreading across the country. At his death, the company went to Beatrice, his wife of more than four decades. Francis had a very sizable trust fund, but his mother controlled the empire. She tolerated Margo but held her in no higher regard than her son's Duesenberg or string of polo ponies. Margo threw herself into the role of belle of endless parties, arousing smiles and leers from wealthy men on the international scene. And so, she bent her knee to Beatrice and bided her time. If she engaged in a dalliance or two along the way, Francis pretended not to notice.

As Francis moved forward, with a bearer on his right, the tall grass swayed like a curtain being drawn, and a huge male water buffalo stalked out. He trotted toward Francis. Wilson left Margo and ran forward to get a good shot, but Francis raised his rifle and fired twice, once hitting the horn above the left eye. The second hit lower and entered the neck. The bull let out a bellow, turned, and ran back into the grass. A cloud of dust and grass stalks flew up as the bull thundered to the ground.

"Good shot," Wilson yelled. "You got him."

Francis wheeled around toward his companions, his rifle raised high above his head.

"I did it," he cried and jumped into a little victory dance.

Francis craned his neck to get a better view of Margo standing next to the Land Rover.

"Hey, Margo, did you see that? Too bad the lion wasn't here

to witness it."

Margo gripped the Mannlicher so tightly her knuckles turned white, as if she were ready to break it over her knee.

The grass swayed again, and the wounded buffalo burst toward Francis. Macomber stood his ground, leveled the rifle, and fired again. Simultaneously, shots rang out from the rifles of Wilson and the bearer. The buffalo skidded to a stop, two meters from Macomber's feet. Then, a second shot from the Mannlicher. Francis felt a sudden white-hot, blinding flash explode inside his head, and that was the last thing he ever felt.

Margo thought of ordering another gimlet but instead dropped her half-smoked cigarette into the empty glass and went back to her room.

The next morning, a taxi with its trunk door missing took her to the Nairobi airport. At the head of the lone runway sat a gray, metal Ford Trimotor with Kenya Airways painted in red on the fuselage. This was not the plane Margo expected, but the gate agent said it was all that was available today, also that it would be making more refueling stops along the way than the other plane. In addition, the gate agent said she would have to pay for a ticket for Francis, even though he would be flying in the luggage compartment. The plane would land somewhere in Ethiopia on its way north to Khartoum, the first leg of her journey to Cairo. Finally, a change of planes for the longer flight up the Nile to Cairo.

At take-off, there were only three other passengers aboard the

Trimotor. A smirk of irony crossed Margo's lips. "Since he had a ticket, Francis could have been up here with the rest of us," she thought.

When the steward came by, she ordered a gimlet.

The Trimotor rattled its way north to the refueling stop in Ethiopia. It was now 1936, and Margo learned the Italians were in charge when a young Italian officer came on board to check everyone's passport. Margo returned his smile, noting how handsome he looked in his uniform.

"Still a baby," she thought, but he'd do.

The officer nodded to her and walked back up the aisle to the exit, the tassel on his cap swinging lasciviously.

Margo was relieved to board a much larger plane in Khartoum. She had stayed on the ground to make sure Francis made it into the cargo hold. Now seated at a window in first class, she watched the blue ribbon of the Nile unfurl beneath her. Once in Cairo, she would board her flight to London with a layover at Paris-Le Bourget.

She nodded off with thoughts of taking a taxi into the City of Lights to the Lapin Agile, the café she had come to love before she met Francis. Hopefully, Henri, the maître d', would still be there, and he would remember her. Henri was a rake, but a man of discretion, and he would guide her to an interesting evening. Francis, of course, would stay behind at the airport in Customs or Baggage Check. Margo would tip the taxi driver handsomely to get her back to Le Bourget in the nick of time to make the morning flight to

London, just like in the old days.

She and Francis would take the train down to Southampton to board Britain's newest liner, the *Queen Mary*, bound for New York on her maiden voyage. Francis's mother had booked the *Queen Mary* the previous year, as a birthday present for her son.

"Perhaps it was better for Francis," Margo thought. Francis felt squeamish about taking an ocean liner across the Atlantic on its maiden voyage.

He thanked his mother profusely for the gift but later told Margo he couldn't get the Titanic out of his mind.

"Oh, rot, my dear," she told him. "This is 1936. Ships don't sink anymore. They've fixed that."

Once they landed in Cairo, everyone deplaned and queued up to go through Customs. When Margo reached the head of the line, a man in uniform came out from behind the desk. He waved her out of the queue with his clipboard, that universal sign of authority.

"You are Margo Macomber?"

Margo beamed, delighted as always to be recognized. It wasn't that long ago that she had graced the cover of British Vogue. Perhaps this official remembered her.

"I am. You are a dear."

"We see you are traveling with personal luggage, a sealed crate, and a long box that appears to be a sarcophagus."

Margo's smile grew cold. She crisply explained that the crate contained a lion skin, head intact, and ready for the taxidermist.

"The long box contains the remains of my husband, killed in a hunting accident. I am taking him back to the United States for his funeral and burial."

"My sympathies for your loss, Ma'am. But we must open all your baggage, including the sarcophagus. The government has found an increase in antiquities being smuggled out of Egypt. We apologize, but these are the regulations."

"Nonsense," she snapped. "I am traveling from Nairobi and just got off the flight from Khartoum. There cannot be anything Egyptian in my belongings. And it's not a sarcophagus, it's the travel casket from the funeral home in Nairobi."

"Things could have been added in Khartoum." The worker bowed in official deference. "Without your knowledge, of course."

He turned with a military about-face and went through the door behind him. Margo watched him walk away, past a soldier with a rifle. She could see the casket at the far end of the room. Two men were standing at the casket, one holding an even larger clipboard and the other a tennis racquet. The guard shut the door, blocking her view into the room.

At the ticket desk, the clerk assured her that, barring any problems, her luggage would be on the flight to Brussels, which was now boarding.

"Brussels? I'm on the plane to Paris."

"My apologies, Ma'am, but the Germans have moved into the Rhineland on the French border, and France has closed every airport from Marseilles to Bordeaux, including Paris. Your flight has been diverted to Brussels.

"Is there a war, then?"

The clerk shrugged and handed Margo her boarding pass.

"Your flight is leaving early before the Belgians decide to close their airports as well." Margo settled into her seat in First Class and immediately ordered a scotch and water.

A steward had assured her that all her luggage, including Francis's casket, was in the cargo hold. She felt both relief and anger: relief that Francis and the lion were on their way to his mother, anger that she would miss spending a layover in Paris.

"Brussels," she sniffed, "only good for beer and chocolates."

A tall man with blonde hair and a ruddy complexion greeted Margo and slipped into the seat next to her. The ruddy cheeks reminded her of Robert Wilson. But she doubted Wilson could ever dress so elegantly, even if he was to be presented at court, an event she could not imagine. He wore a well-pressed suit of expensive Italian design, with vest and tie, even a tie tack and pocket square. How he managed to look so collected in the blistering Cairo heat amazed Margo, who was rarely prone to amazement.

"This bears further examination," she thought.

The gentleman introduced himself as Harry Lawson, an agent of the British Consulate in New York. He got straight to the heart of what matters to Margo by adding, "And you must be Margo Macomber."

"A pleasure to meet you, Mr. Lawson," she said and extended her hand.

Lawson held her hand for what Margo considered a bit longer

than a cordial greeting might require, and she felt a warm thrill of connection.

"How did you recognize me?" she asked. Suddenly, she turned cold. Could the story of Francis's demise, and her possible involvement, have reached the international press? After all, a photographer was snapping away as she and Robert Wilson left the courthouse after the inquest. It had been years since she had a publicist who would have given her the clippings immediately.

"Oh, I remember you from the covers of fashion magazines."

Margo beamed and conjured up a sly smile, her trademark look. They exchanged the usual opening lines of travelers upon a first meeting. After the diversion to Brussels, they would both take a plane to London.

"Then, the train down to Southampton to board the *Queen Mary* to return to New York," she said.

"What a coincidence," Lawson replied, with no attempt to hide his delight. "I am going back the same way. It's the liner's maiden voyage, you know."

"Coincidence? Is he following me? Does he know about Francis?" she thought.

Margo dismissed the idea as something that crops up as one ages, and she would have none of it. The possibility of a liaison amoureuse with Harry Lawson wiped away her suspicions.

"You are traveling alone?" he asked.

"No, my husband is with me."

Margo was assured by the look of dismay that crossed Lawson's face.

"He is in the cargo hold. In a casket. I am taking his body back to his mother in Connecticut. We will hold the funeral there on the family estate."

Lawson's condolences gushed forth, ending with the question, "How did he…" he searched for a word, "…pass?"

"Hunting accident. We were on safari in Kenya."

She gave him the doe-eyed innocent look she had used in the two-page spread for Pond's Night Crème.

"I'd rather not talk about it right now."

Lawson sat back in his seat and looked straight ahead.

"I'm terribly sorry," he whispered.

After a moment, Margo took his arm and leaned her head on his shoulder. They remained in that position for the rest of the flight. They even passed up lunch.

They arrived in Brussels in barely enough time to catch the flight to London. At the gate, the ticket agent expressed his condolences to Margo and assured her that the casket was being treated with respect.

Margo took Harry's arm and murmured her regrets that they hadn't had the time for him to buy her a box of chocolates.

"Or for you to get me a bottle of beer," he whispered.

They had lunch at Heathrow Aerodrome before hiring a taxi to take them to the boat train to Southampton, where the *Queen Mary* was docked. The driver grumbled and had to get help with lashing the casket to the top of the cab. Harry tipped him well, and the lion rode up front. As the boat train pulled out for Southampton, Margo grumbled about not being able to spend a day in Paris.

"Those damn Germans ruined everything," she said. What in the world are they doing in France?"

"Actually, they marched into Germany," he replied and held forth with a scholarly explanation of the retaking of the Rhineland, which was historically German territory but ceded to France as part of the reparations after the Great War.

"So, you see," he concluded, "Germany is simply reclaiming what they feel is rightfully theirs. Pity," he sighed, "and just when the Olympics are about to start in Berlin."

"Well, it's all a bother," she huffed. "I've missed my chance to see the Lapin Agile again and my beautiful friend Henri, the maître d' there."

Harry gripped her hand. "I'm afraid Henri is dead."

She looked at him and shook her head as if to rattle some sense into what she had just heard.

"I'm sorry, my dear. I know the Lapin Agile well. I lived in Paris for a number of years. You are one of many who knew Henri, such a sweet man. His death was sudden and tragic."

Harry leaned closer and whispered, "I won't give you the details, even though it was in all the papers. It's best if you remember Henri as he was in the café, which is what I have been trying to do."

He kissed her on the cheek, and she pulled him close, and their lips met. For a moment, both Henri and Francis faded into a dream.

The *Queen Mary* presented a magnificent sight, towering over the dockside offices and cavernous waiting area. Margo and Harry presented their own sight to the crowds of passengers, well-wishers, and the curious. The couple walked up the gangway followed by porters carrying their luggage, the casket, and in its wooden crate, the lion. Margo had made arrangements to have Francis and the lion placed in her stateroom, a two-room suite that was as large as one found in a luxury hotel. Harry had booked a stateroom on the deck below, which he planned on not using.

The departure was all fireworks, foghorns and flash powder. Photographers and newsreel cameramen elbowed each other to get the best shot. Margo waved from the railing, striking pose after pose, hoping for a magazine cover or a front page. Perhaps, even a few seconds on Movietone News.

The first leg of the voyage was a short one, across the Channel to Cherbourg, to allow French, Belgian, and Dutch dignitaries to depart. They had played their part on the speakers' platform and were now being returned like borrowed merchandise.

At dinner in one of the gilded dining rooms, Margo and Harry were seated with an American couple, a man with extremely large ears, and his wife, wearing a now out-of-date hat from the flapper era. Large Ears revealed he was an insurance executive with a firm in Baltimore. His wife was there to support his stories and inject what Margo felt were unnecessary details.

Not wanting to be steamrolled with anecdotes about the insurance business, Margo asked Large Ears if he knew of Beatrice

Macomber and Kenilworth Holdings.

"Oh, everyone knows of Kenilworth Holdings. Does your mother-in-law work for them?"

"She owns it," Margo replied and gazed at him over the rim of her scotch and water.

Flapper Hat cooed like a pigeon, and Large Ears grunted in acknowledgement before jumping to another topic.

"Rumor going 'round that when we docked to let the bigwigs off, two or three hundred Jews came aboard." Large Ears leaned forward and whispered, "Fleeing Germany for America."

"You don't say," Harry responded,

"Like rats leaving a sinking ship," Large Ears declared.

"And what would that sinking ship be?" Howard asked.

"Why, Germany, of course."

Harry took a sip of wine. "The majority of Germans don't feel that way. They see it rising."

"The majority of Germans are fools, then," Large Ears smirked.

"We shall see," Harry replied.

Large Ears turned to Margo. "What do you think, Mrs. Macomber?"

Margo looked into her scotch. "I have no opinion. But I loved Berlin. That was back in the twenties."

"Oh, the twenties," Flapper Hat cooed. "That was my time."

"No doubt," Margo said.

The first night, Harry displayed his chivalry by walking Margo to her stateroom. She asked him in. He followed her to the bedroom. He could see the casket through the door to the next room. She turned to him, grabbed his lapels, and pulled him down onto the bed with her.

"Won't this feel a bit odd with your husband in the next room?" he whispered.

She cocked her head and smiled, "It won't be the first time."

The Cunard Lines brochure promised the *Queen Mary* would make the crossing from Southampton to New York in seven nights. Margo and Harry would have preferred eight or ten.

A few nights later, after a stroll around the third deck, Margo and Harry dropped into one of the lounges available to First Class passengers. Sitting at a table in a far corner were Large Ears and two other men. Large Ears motioned them over.

"We were thinking about a friendly game of poker. Care to join us?" he asked.

"Why not?" Margo responded. "I'm feeling competitive to-night."

The couple took seats opposite each other.

Large Ears riffled the deck. "The game is draw poker, aces high, deuces and black queens wild, with a two-hundred-dollar buy-in."

A flurry of bills landed in the middle of the table.

"I'll pay for the lady," Harry said, "and peeled four hundred-dollar bills from a wad in his pocket and tossed them into the mix.

Margo nodded to him. "Thanks, this should be a fun night."

After several hands, the largest number of chips sat in front of Harry. Margo had been dealt some good hands but misplayed them when there was a chance of Harry winning. She thought it would be advantageous to pump him up for later in the evening.

Large Ears talked throughout the game, once leaning forward conspiratorially to divulge another rumor.

"Word's going around that a submarine surfaced not two hundred yards off the port side yesterday. Then, it disappeared."

One of the players, a Canadian with a bushy moustache, snorted, "What would a submarine be doing way out here?"

Harry stretched and stifled a yawn. "Probably looking for icebergs. From under the surface, of course."

Margo and Harry arrived back at her stateroom in time to meet a steward delivering a cablegram for her. Once inside, she opened the envelope. It was from Beatrice.

SENDING CAR AND DRIVER TO MEET YOU AT DOCK STOP ALSO HEARSE FROM WENTWORTH MORTUARY STOP WILL AWAIT YOU AT HOUSE STOP B

"Well, looks like his mother is sparing no expense," she said. "Wentworth's buries only the finest people in Connecticut."

She yelled toward the next room. "Francis, looks like you're still going first class."

"I'm going with you to Connecticut," Harry said. His voice

was firm.

"That's impossible," she said. "How would it look if I showed up at my newly deceased husband's funeral with a boyfriend?"

"I've thought about it, and here's my plan."

Margo sighed and sank onto the edge of the bed. "Go ahead, I'm listening."

"Kenya is a British colony, and I am with the British Consulate. It's part of official protocol that someone in authority accompanies the deceased and his widow back to their home. Your mother-in-law has simplified our situation by sending transportation. You will ride in the car with the driver, and I will ride in the hearse. Once we arrive, we will sort things out. I will stay in a hotel, and you will be the grieving widow at the Macomber estate."

Margo beamed and shook her head in appreciation.

"And I will stay at my home on the river and sneak away to meet you at the hotel. Book a room at the Statler; it's the largest in town, and we can be very anonymous. When things die down, you can move into my house, and we can be together."

Margo and Francis's house was three miles from the Macomber estate, and in contrast, very modern.

"Beatrice calls it a monstrosity," she said with a wicked laugh.

"Good. I love monstrosities," he said

Margo rose from the chair, shut the door to the adjoining room, and seemed to float into his open arms.

The *Queen Mary* arrived in New York harbor amidst fireworks and geysers from fireboats. The dock swarmed with photographers and newsreel cameramen in a replay of the joyous tumult the liner had enjoyed at her send-off in Southampton.

Two men that Harry said were from the Consulate helped the entourage — Margo, Harry, Francis, the lion, and three baggage handlers — down the gangway and into Customs. Thanks to the turmoil caused by crowds of greeters and gawkers and an ocean liner full of disembarking passengers, the overburdened Customs agents simply waved Margo's group through.

True to Beatrice's promise, the hearse and car, a brand-new royal blue 1936 Packard sedan, were waiting. And true to Harry's plan, Margo got into the Packard, and Harry slid into the front seat of the hearse. Once out of Manhattan, it was a speedy trip to their destination, a few miles outside of Hartford. Homes in that area didn't have addresses, only titles: Rockcrest, Falconshire, and Sans Sucie, all borrowed from the French, and all spelled incorrectly. The Macomber mansion was named Valhalla, or as the locals called it, "the Macomber place."

Valhalla was an imposing castle-like structure, befitting the late Roderick Macomber, who made his millions in real estate and insurance. The Great Depression passed over Valhalla like the Angel of Death over the Israelites. Roderick Macomber would have objected to such a comparison, as the two country clubs to which he belonged boasted restricted memberships.

Harry, the driver of the hearse, and two Valhalla staff acted as pallbearers, carrying the casket up the granite steps and into the grand hall. The traveling casket was slim and simple and could easily have been carried by only two men.

Beatrice rushed forward to greet her returning son, leaning on the casket and sobbing even before the bearers could set it down on the brass trestle wheeled out to accommodate it. A few yards behind the trestle loomed what would be the official casket, all mahogany and brass with a golden angel at each corner.

Margo stood at the foot of the casket, waiting for Beatrice to stand erect, so that she could offer condolences and perhaps even share a hug. Harry lingered in the background so as not to show any familiarity with Margo.

Tears and hugs having been accomplished, Beatrice ordered the coffin to be opened so she could see her son, her only child. Mr. Wentworth, the head of the funeral home, tried to dissuade her from seeing the corpse until Francis was properly installed in the mahogany Grand Star: Traveler to Eternity, as his top-of-the-line casket was called.

Beatrice would not be deterred.

While an assistant from the funeral home worked on the latches holding the lid in place, Margo stepped forward to hug the bereaved mother. Harry could see real tears in Margo's eyes.

As the lid was raised, Harry motioned to Margo to step back. Who knew how skilled the Kenyan mortician was at embalming? Harry covered his nose with his pocket square.

Fully opened, the casket revealed an almost perfectly preserved Francis Macomber. And no discernible smell.

Beatrice fell on her son, covering his cheeks and lips with kisses. People rushed forward to keep Beatrice from falling farther into the coffin. During the tumult, a tall man wearing a tweed blazer and silver tie stepped to the foot of the casket. He reached in and pulled something from beneath Francis's feet. It was a tennis racquet. The silver-tied man quickly stuffed the racquet into a leather bag and nodded to a heavy-set man standing with him. Margo shot a bewildered glance at Harry, who merely shrugged and refolded his pocket square.

Once Beatrice was pulled back from the coffin, Harry went to her and expressed his condolences on behalf of the British Consulate in New York. He turned and walked briskly to the door, stopping by Margo to give her a formal handshake. Then, he jogged down the granite steps and into a waiting taxi.

When Margo got to Harry's room at the Statler, she found the door unlocked.

"Must be eager to see me," she thought. "How sweet."

Harry was bent over his briefcase on the bed. An unopened suitcase lay next to it. He walked quickly to her, planted a very functional kiss on her cheek, and returned to the other side of the bed. An uneasy feeling rose from the pit of her stomach.

"Is something wrong?"

Harry motioned to the armchair next to her. "Please sit down. I have a confession to make to you. It may take a few minutes."

"You're married," she responded. Her tone was flat and louder than she had expected.

"Not as simple as that." He drew a deep breath and fixed his eyes on hers.

"First of all, I find myself falling in love with you, but the timing is not right. I am not who I said I was. I am not with the British Consulate. It's actually the German Consulate. I am not British. I am German, and my name is Heinrich. Ich bin Deutsche."

He paused to see how Margo would react to this revelation. She did not blink.

"I must go to New York tonight to be briefed on my next assignment."

"So, I am being dumped again," she said with just a trace of bitterness.

"You see, I am dedicated to a cause that will result in a new Germany."

Margo stared at him. "You are a Nazi, then?"

"Being a member of the Party is a requirement for employment, I'm afraid. Some of us don't believe in that strutting little fool. We see him as what you would call a 'necessary evil' for the restoration of Germany to its former glory, indeed for its evolution into a power we have not previously known. Herr Hitler will cause turmoil, probably go to war, and eventually see the German people turn against him. Our goal is a greater Germany once the Führer is swept from the scene."

"That's all rot," she said. "And to think I trusted you."

"You have a good heart, which leads you to be too trusting. Surely, you knew your late husband was one of us."

"What are you saying? Francis?"

"Your jaunts around the world?" Harry leaned across the bed toward her. "Francis was a courier for us. Imagine how many rolls of microfilm were hidden in the handles of his tennis racquets. The latest mission was to bring a copy of a secret code here to America to be used by our allies here."

Harry felt energized by his decision to share his story with a woman he loved but might not see ever again.

"More German agents like you, then," she said.

"No, Americans. Hundreds of organizations working for our cause. Remember the man wearing the silver tie? That was William Pelley, the leader of the Silver Shirts, a pro-Nazi group working for us. And the fat man next to him? An emissary from Father Coughlin, the radio priest who rails against F.D.R."

"But the tennis racquet wasn't Francis's. He would never use a Wilson."

"Because of Francis's untimely death, we had to improvise. It was the only racquet we could find in Cairo. Putting it in the casket was a last-minute move."

"I'm feeling overwhelmed," Margo said and buried her head in her hands. Through her fingers, she asked, "Did his mother know about this?"

" Yes, she did." Harry felt another thrill as he prepared for the next revelation.

"Beatrice Macomber funded the whole operation. She is a major fundraiser for the Party. You can be sure that this was not the first time Pelley and Coughlin's major domo had been to the Macomber estate."

"That bitch," she hissed. "And her son…" Her voice trailed off into sobs.

Harry snapped his briefcase shut and picked up his suitcase.

"I will leave you now before I decide that I cannot leave you ever," he said as he opened the door. "My fondest wish is that we meet again after all this is over."

He closed the door behind him.

Margo sat motionless in the armchair, thoughts whirling through her head. She noticed that the sun had gone down, and the only light came from the table lamp beside her. As the hours passed, her whirling thoughts wafted into dreams of planes and trains and lions. When she awoke, her face was damp with tears. "No, I don't cry. I don't," she said aloud. "Time to get started."

Margo marched into the bathroom and stood in front of the mirror. She did not like what she saw. She wiped away the mascara that had run down to her chin, washed her face, and reapplied her makeup: Coty No. 9 foundation, No. 17 blush, and a dab of Evening in Paris on neck and wrists. The mirror told her she was ready to face the world.

Margo returned to the armchair. She remembered attending one of Beatrice's fundraising galas in some hotel ballroom. While Francis stood at the bar, she struck up a conversation with a rather good-looking, well-put-together gentleman. Perhaps out of boredom, perhaps feeling her second glass of champagne, she began to flirt with him. She flashed several of her magazine-cover smiles, and he responded. The tête-à-tête ended when she caught Francis frowning at her from the bar. She excused herself, but not before the gentleman slipped her his card. "Riley J. Withers. Agent in Charge. Federal Bureau of Investigation, Manhattan District," along with address and phone number. There was a phone on the table next to her. She picked it up and asked the operator to be connected to the FBI in Manhattan.

Withers remembered her and, after hearing her story, asked her to come down to his office immediately.

Margo pointed the Packard toward New York City and brushed away a few stray tears as she drove. She gripped the wheel so tightly that her knuckles turned white and achy.

"No one dumps Margo Macomber," she whispered. "No one."

THEA AND FRITZ: BERLIN 1931–1933

Prologue: Berlin 1952

I couldn't help fingering the plastic bag in my coat pocket as I walked down a dingy street in a West Berlin warehouse district. Forty grams of high-quality cocaine I bought in Amsterdam from a dealer I trusted. Kleinheinz said Walter would let me see his uncle's collection of old movie posters for the forty grams. But I couldn't let the uncle know. How could I? I doubt I'd ever meet the guy, unless it was at a convention of collectors of rare posters. I never talk about my own collection. Too risky to be tracked down and burglarized, or held in a warehouse, like one of these, and tortured until I gave them the whereabouts of my posters.

I flew into West Berlin from Amsterdam, landing at Tempelhof. After dropping my bag at a worn-down hotel, I took a taxi to the grimy warehouse district and my target, Berganalee 614. I rang the bell, and after a pause long enough for me to smoke half a cigarette, the door opened and a short man with watery eyes and a scruffy beard appeared in what was left of the sunlight.

"Walter?" I asked.

"Who are you?"

"I'm Traeger, Kleinheinz said you had something for me to see."

"You bring the entrance fee?" he asked, eyeing me up and down.

I pulled out the plastic bag and waved it under his nose.

"Come in. It better be good stuff."

"Have a taste," I said.

Walter opened the bag and stuck a wet, grimy finger inside. He licked his finger and smacked his lips like a child reaching into the cake batter.

"Not bad."

I followed Walter down a dimly lit hallway and into a maze of narrower passages until we reached a large commercial freezer that smelled of leaking Freon and rotting meat. Walter turned a key in the lock hanging from the freezer handles.

"God, those posters are going to stink," I thought.

But the freezer was only the first step. Walter unlocked another door set into the wall behind the freezer. He turned on a light inside to reveal a hidden room and motioned me to follow him through the freezer and into the dimness. I flashed on *The Cask of Amontillado*, where the host bricks up his unsuspecting visitor in a cellar wall. I have an artist's proof of the poster for the Spanish language version of the film, which starred Vincent Price and Peter Lorre.

My host sidled between two stacks of cardboard cartons to a bank of wide, flat drawers that might hold maps or architectural drawings. Or, I hoped, posters.

Walter pulled open the top drawer, and there they were, interspersed between sheets of anti-acid paper, a stack of antique cinema posters. Walter pulled off the top protective sheet to reveal what looked to be an artist's proof of the poster for the original 1920s version of *Nosferatu*. As a fan of vampire films, I already had this one, and in better condition.

"There are hundreds here. My uncle's collection is quite extensive, from the 1910s to around 1950, when he seemed to lose interest in the newer posters."

Walter excused himself while he lay out a line of coke and snorted it through a short piece of soda straw.

"Feel free to look through all of them," he said. Then, he sneezed and wiped his nose on his sleeve.

I started to reach into the drawer, but Walter pulled back my arm. He waved a pair of rubber gloves under my nose.

"You must wear these while you handle them."

"Of course," I said and pulled the gloves on.

"Actually, I'm looking for some posters from Fritz Lang's films."

Walter slammed the open drawer shut with such force that I was afraid I'd offended him.

"What?" I thought. "Because Lang had left Germany for Hollywood?"

Walter bent down and opened a drawer near the bottom of the chest.

"I think you'll find him here," he said and removed the top sheet of protective paper.

Walter stood over me as I crouched down to have a look. I suddenly felt vulnerable. Here I was in a warehouse in a deserted neighborhood, having stepped through a gutted freezer and into a secret room with a coke addict I had just met — with him standing over me wearing rubber gloves. What else was in that stack of cartons? Body parts?

"Be my guest," Walter said and stepped away. I could hear him preparing to have another snort off the poster case. I started to leaf through the stack of posters. The top one was a prize, a poster for one of Lang's most famous films, *Metropolis* from 1927, a look into the future, with robots and a rebellion of the working class. In pristine condition with Director Fritz Lang, and Writers Lang and Thea von Harbou in bold letters. It was in far better condition than the one in my collection.

"I'll take this one," I yelled over my shoulder and handed it up to Walter. "I'll keep going," I said.

Fritz Lang and Thea von Harbou were married and formed the most famous and successful directing/writing team in Germany in the Twenties and early Thirties. The hair stood up on the back of my neck at the thought of finding others by this duo.

Farther down were posters from Lang's Hollywood years, *Fury, Man Hunt, Western Union,* and *Cloak and Dagger* with Gary Cooper. I had all of them, so I dug down farther.

Then, I hit paydirt. *Das Indische Grabmal.* My hands trembled as I held the poster for what translated to *The Indian Grave,* with both Lang and von Harbou credited for the screenplay, adapted from her novel. A double win for von Harbou, I thought. The film was a reflection of both Lang and von Harbou's passion for Indian art and culture. It would add great value to my collection.

"I'll take this one, too," I said, trying to throttle my excitement.

Digging further, I came to the last poster and had trouble unsticking it from its acid-free paper cover. Lying at the bottom of the drawer with the weight of the others pressing down on it, the cover fused with the poster's ink in several places. It took all I had to gently pry them apart. And there it was, the one I searched for years to find. The Lang/von Harbou thriller, whose title was but a single letter, M. M for Murder, based on true events surrounding the pursuit of a child murderer. The film gave stage actor Peter Lorre recognition throughout Europe.

I handed the poster up to Walter. "And this one, too," summoning all the nonchalance I could muster.

Walter seemed uninterested in my choices, having snorted a second line while I was digging. He rolled up the posters, careful to sandwich them with the sheets of paper, and tied them with a length of yellow ribbon he pulled out of God knows where.

"That'll be three hundred," he said, adding "U.S."

I reached for my wallet, took out three one-hundred-dollar bills, and handed them to him. He glanced at them, wiped his nose on his sleeve again, and stuffed them into his shirt pocket. Given the fragility of West German currency, U.S. cash was the preferred mode of exchange.

He escorted me out of the room, through the freezer, and out to the street. I turned to thank him, but the door clanked shut, and he disappeared. I walked down to Kurfürstendamm, hailed a taxi, and went back to my hotel.

I unrolled the posters on the bed and allowed myself to gloat over the best acquisition I had ever made in the shortest amount of time. I planned to take a flight from Tempelhof back to Amsterdam in the morning, gripping the roll of posters all the way.

Gazing at the poster for M, I mused over what I knew about Fritz and Thea's fraught relationship and their work together. I had researched their lives and conjured up a story that held together tentatively, like fragments of an ancient scroll with pieces missing, blanks begging to be filled in. Their story is perhaps best presented as a reel of film, each scene a fragment from a scroll that unrolled in Berlin from 1931 to 1933.

Scene 1. Thea and Fritz's Berlin Apartment. 1931.
Since both were devotees of Indian art and culture, the apartment is adorned with copies of Indian artifacts – paintings, sculptures, etc. (Their official position was that these were mere copies.) Hanging in the background is a large painting of Shiva as Lord of the Dance. A couch is festooned with brightly colored Indian scarves. Nearby, an elegantly carved table with a typewriter, notebooks, and stacks of paper. Thea is at the typewriter, and Fritz lolls on the couch. He has worked his way up the ranks, beginning as an actor and screenwriter, until his directorial talent made him one of the most successful auteurs in German cinema. He wears a patch over his right eye, lost while serving in the Austrian army in the First World War.

Fritz erupts impatiently, "All right, now read Beckert's speech to me again."

Thea reads from a page of the script, "You are proud of being able to crack into safes or cheat at cards. All of which, it seems to me, you could just as easily give up, if you had learned something useful, if you were not such lazy pigs."

"That should get us past the censors," Fritz says. The criminals pursue crime because they are lazy, not because they are out of work."

Both are aware that they must take any focus away from increased unemployment in Berlin, which the National Socialists are sensitive to.

"Let's change the title, as well," Fritz suggests.

"You think A City Searches for a Murderer is still too strong?"

"Definitely. And it's too long."

"Then let's make it as short as possible," Thea suggests. "One letter – M."

Fritz ponders her suggestion. "M?"

"Yes, M – for murder or murderer."

"One letter – M. Memorable. I can see it on cinema marquees everywhere – Fritz Lang's M."

Thea cuts in with a sigh, "Screenplay by Thea von Harbou and Fritz Lang."

"The credit will be on the posters," he replies.

"Of course. I'm just not a marquee kind of girl."

Lang met von Harbou in 1920, shortly after his first wife died under mysterious circumstances. She was found in a bathtub, dead from a gunshot wound. Lang and von Harbou, who were a couple at the time, were exonerated, even though the gun in question was Lang's World War I service revolver. They married in 1922, and she either wrote or co-wrote every Lang/von Harbou film until 1933. Von Harbou has been described as a child prodigy, writing poems and short stories from an early age, as well as being drawn to writing epic myths and legends with an overtly nationalistic tone. She became a popular novelist, but this work diminished as she became increasingly involved in screenwriting. She was an extremely attractive woman, arguably the reason Lang was drawn to her.

Lang pulls a letter from his pocket.

"I have a surprise for you, a piece of good news. Here are the signed contracts, one with Otto Wernicke, who will play the Inspector, and the other with Peter Lorre. He'll be our murderer, our 'M'."

"Peter Lorre. He's perfect for the part, a dream come true." Thea gushes like a teenager. "Those bulging eyes. I can see him now in close-up. He looks for all the world like a killer of little girls. But he's a Jew. Isn't he?"

"He's an Austrian," Fritz replies. "So, I suppose he is a Jew, as am I."

"You are not a Jew."

"Certainly, I am an Austrian and a Jew."

"You're a Catholic. Not a very good one, to be sure, but still a Catholic."

"Thea, for the hundredth time, my mother was Jewish, so that makes me a Jew, despite her conversion to all that Romish fol-de-rol. Now, you can meet with Wernicke and tell him we start shooting next Thursday. Lorre will be at the studio, too. He's beyond excited that his first film role will be in Germany's first talkie."

There is a knock at the door, and Thea rushes to answer it. It is Ayi Tendulkar, a tall, swarthy Indian journalist. He is in Gandhi's circle and in Berlin to lobby for Germany to aid India in its coming struggle for independence. He is 27, and despite their sixteen-year age difference — or perhaps because of it — Thea has begun a clandestine affair with him. No matter: Lang has a reputation as a rake. One of his several lovers was the leading actress in his last two films, *Spione (The Spies)* and *Frau im Mond (Woman in the Moon)*, both written by Lang and von Harbou. Lang's current lover is the actress Lily Latté.

Thea welcomes him warmly as he pushes a small, wheeled table into the room. On top of the table is the latest model record player, another feat of German engineering.

Ayi presses his palms together, bowing to each of them. "My apologies for interrupting, but I have a gift for you that cannot wait." He scurries around to find a wall socket and plugs in the record player.

"That's all right," Lang says with less-than-mild sarcasm, "we were just in the middle of an important meeting, is all."

Thea shushes her husband and giggles, "Ayi, you are a dear. What have you brought us?"

"We already have a gramophone," Lang says wearily.

"With your permission, the Indian community in Berlin has brought you a token of our thanks for your friendship and assistance with our cultural affairs."

"You are most welcome," Thea says and sweeps her arm to indicate the collection of Indian art in the room. "You can see we are devotees of the art of your country."

"And you shall have more," says Ayi, with an undisguised wink at Thea. He turns on the record player and drops the arm on the record inside. Immediately, the room is filled with music played on traditional Indian instruments, sitar, tabla, and tamboura. A dancer in traditional dress, including ankle bells, floats through the door and performs a short classical Indian dance. She finishes by striking a pose, then dances out the door.

Thea applauds the performance enthusiastically, Lang less so.

"Thank you so much," Ayi responds with a deep bow. "This is but a preview of the concert of classical dance we shall be presenting in two months' time. The community is inviting both of you to be our guests of honor. Please, say you will come."

"Of course we will. We'll be delighted, won't we, Fritz?"

"If we are not shooting a film, then."

"If we're still shooting M, my dear, we'll be over budget and in the poor house."

"True enough," Lang sighs. "Ayi, we'll be there. Just give us a firm date."

"I will. Thank you so much, Herr Lang."

Ayi glides over to Thea and kisses her on the cheek. "And thank you, too, my muse."

He wheels the record player to the door, turns and bows, palms together, and disappears into the hall.

Fritz turns to the script papers on the desk and, feigning nonchalance, asks, "What is this 'muse' business?"

"Oh, he's been reading my novels. He says they inspire him. Ach, what a puppy."

"Just so he doesn't bite."

"You should talk."

"Enough. Now, where were we?"

"You are going to see the set designer, and I am to meet with Wernicke."

"You can see him tomorrow. You need to get these rewrites to the copyist."

Thea gathers up the script papers and stuffs them into an envelope. "I can do both today. There's still time. Tomorrow I'm speaking at the rally."

"The rally?"

"The rally against Paragraph 218. We can't allow those graybeards at the Reichstag to make abortion a crime. I'm going to add my voice to the opposition."

"Once again, you're poking the hornet's nest, setting us up to have our M film scrutinized.

Thea picks up her hat and purse with an air of, and that's that. "The Reichstag is hardly a hornet's nest — more like a nest of drones. They tremble at the thought of being supplanted by the Communists or the National Socialists."

Thea leaves, slamming the door behind her. Lang follows and shouts into the hall, "Tell him I expect a great performance from him. He'd better be Lorre's equal."

Scene 2. A Berlin Art Gallery – 1931

An opening cocktail party is in progress. The show features the work of caricaturist "Dolbin." He is known for skewering politicians and the rich, both Left and Right. Guests, in twos and threes, are holding wine glasses, engaging in polite conversation, from which bursts of laughter emanate from time to time. The walls are lined with framed Dolbin works in pen-and-ink. Hanging above is one large poster displaying an enlarged caricature with the title of the show in three languages: Kunstwerke von Dolbin – Oeuvres de Dolbin – Works of Dolbin.

The atmosphere is friendly and relaxed, as these people are part of the arts scene and know each other. Guests include artist Benedict Dolbin, gallery owner Maria Brueken, Fritz Lang and Thea von Harbou, Ayi Tendulkar, and others. Ayi, as a diversion from being there to see Thea, flirts with a pretty girl as they admire the caricatures.

Maria pulls Lang aside and chides him, "Come now, Herr Lang, surely you can tell me about the film you and Thea are working on."

"I'm sorry, Maria, but we cannot divulge it just yet. Thea and

I have just finished the script."

"Just a hint, then?"

"Sorry. *Es tut mir leid, Liebchen,* as my mother would have said."

"Thea wouldn't tell me anything either. I've never known her to be so tight-lipped."

"Let me say this," Fritz answers with a wink. "It's not about robots. We've moved on from our Metropolis days."

"Yet you were quite the visionary to stare into the future to show flying cars, monstrous machines, and the proletariat rebelling against the elite. I doubt you could make that sort of movie today," Maria says.

"True, unfortunately," Lang agrees, "One would have to be more symbolic."

Dolbin strolls over to join the group. "Well, well, well," Fritz booms, "It's our guest of honor. Congratulations, Benedict, on your show here. All of Berlin admires your work."

"All of Germany," Maria adds.

Dolbin shakes his head sadly. "Not all of Germany, I'm afraid. Some find it, shall we say, incorrect. Corrupting, even. I've been kicked out of the German Press Association and limited to publishing no more than four drawings per month."

Lang pretends to be shocked. "So that's why I've been missing you in my morning paper. You see, Maria, it's this atmosphere that makes us play our cards close. You are very brave to hold this exhibit for our dear Dolbin."

"It's my duty," Maria says. "Dolbin is a treasure."

"A Jewish treasure," Dolbin emphasizes.

"An international treasure," Lang adds.

"I second that," says Maria, "but I must break off to mingle."

Dolbin calls her back. "One more thing, Maria. If we have any buyers tonight, tell them I will have their purchases delivered to their homes tomorrow. No sense having anyone leave with a piece of my work. They don't need the trouble."

Maria nods and moves to join another group as Thea walks over.

Lang greets his wife warmly and emphasizes her married name for the benefit of Ayi, who is standing nearby. "Join us, Frau Lang. I was just flattering Benedict here."

"No, Fritz," she teases, "this is a working party for him, so we must use his pen name. Isn't that right, 'Dolbin'?"

"Quite so," he replies. "Yes, Dolbin, my pen-and-ink name."

"I think your sales are going well," Lang reassures. "People are eager to purchase caricatures of their enemies."

Dolbin chuckles at the thought. "Just so my friends remember that ten thousand marks equals what one hundred was in the old days. But these are new days. So, Thea, can you persuade Fritz to divulge the nature of your next film?"

Ayi Tendulkar joins the group. He carries a notepad and a pencil.

Fritz welcomes him with somewhat overblown friendliness. "Herr Dolbin, this is our friend Ayi Tendulkar. He poses as a journalist, but his mission is to persuade our country to take up the cause of a free India."

Ayi bows and presses his palms together, scrunching the notepad and pencil. "Herr Dolbin, I am a great admirer of your work."

"*Danke sehr.* So, your job is to spit in the face of the British lion. They won't give up India without a fight."

"Duly noted. But tonight, I am working in ink, not spit. I am writing a review of your show for a newspaper."

"He writes for The Red Flag, among others," Thea adds. "Truly a gifted writer."

Ayi bows to her. "You are too kind."

"No, she's not," Lang grumps. "Underneath it all, she can be a shrew."

Thea responds edgily, "And you would know why, wouldn't you? I suppose Fraulein Latté treats you better."

"Enough," Lang hisses.

"She is your favorite cup of coffee, isn't she?"

Dolbin cuts in to turn the attention to Ayi. "My new friend, I was trying to get our illustrious cinema team to divulge what their next film is about."

"It's a murder mystery," Lang answers, gathering himself.

"It's about a killer of children who is hunted down in the streets of Berlin," Thea adds. "It's based on the acts of serial killer Peter Kurten, the 'Vampire of Düsseldorf,' a decade ago."

"Not necessarily him," corrects Lang. "There are lots of serial killers in Germany. But someone in the censorship bureau got hold of our original script. A member of the National Socialists thought the story was really about them, and, suddenly, the studio decided we couldn't shoot it there, so we found another studio. Please don't ask me where. And that's all we can tell you."

"Who will play the part of the killer?" Dolbin asks.

Before Lang can answer, a clamor erupts at the gallery entrance. Maria taps a knife on a wine glass and calls for attention.

"Ladies and gentlemen, your attention, please," she announces. "We have two surprise guests who have stopped by to wish our gallery well."

Hermann Göring and his companion, the actress Emmy Sonnemann, appear in the doorway. He wears his SA-Gruppenführer jacket adorned with medals. She is dressed in an elegant gown, complemented by furs and pearls. She would later become his second wife.

"May I present Gruppenführer Hermann Göring and his companion, Fräulein Emmy Sonnemann."

Göring fills the room with his presence, and the assemblage stands as if frozen.

"Good evening, my friends," Göring booms. "Let us not interrupt your festivities. Fräulein Sonnemann and I were passing by, and we thought we'd stop in and wish our old friend Dolbin well."

"Thank God my portrait of him wasn't included in the show," Dolbin whispers.

"Don't worry," Fritz says, "You can bet that its absence has already been reported to him."

"Hard to say what might hurt his ego more; it being here or not being here," Thea muses.

Göring and Emmy greet the guests with handshakes and hugs as they work their way toward Dolbin, Ayi, Fritz, and Thea.

"My dear Dolbin," Göring says. "Congratulations on finding a gallery to show your work. I'm a great fan, you know. And Herr Lang and Fräulein von Harbou, I admire your work, as well."

"Thank you, Gruppenführer," Dolbin coughs, as if to keep the words from sticking in his throat.

"We are honored that you came," adds Thea.

Lang stares at Göring but says nothing.

"It is my pleasure. Now, if you'll excuse me, I must speak to our hostess. I have an announcement to make that will excite you as lovers of art."

Göring leaves the group and walks over to Maria. Emmy stays behind.

"I, too, am a great admirer of the work of all of you. Herr Lang, I'm waiting to star in your next film."

"I'm afraid you would find our next one beneath your talents, but perhaps the one after that."

"Marvelous. I'll hold you to it. And Thea, I've been enthralled by your novels. I've read them all. What a gift you have." Emmy gushed.

"Thank you. I loved you in *Schlageter*. What a powerful performance you gave."

"I was stirred by the message of the play," says Emmy. "The

theatre needs to do more to counter the Communist threat before it overwhelms us. But you must excuse me, as I should stand with Gruppenführer Göring."

Emmy leaves the group to join Göring, who stands next to Maria.

"Completely overblown, both the play and her performance," Thea whispers.

Maria taps her glass for attention. "Ladies and gentlemen, once more, your attention. Herr Göring has some news for us."

Göring spreads his arms, like a rotund Jesus addressing his flock. "My friends and fellow art lovers, I am pleased to announce that, come December, my home will be open for an exhibition showing my collection of the finest artworks from across Germany and the world. I have overseen the gathering of paintings and sculpture from private collections far and wide, all of which can now be brought out of hiding and into the light for all the German people to enjoy and admire."

The room fills with applause and a hum of conversation, although some individuals withhold any indication of approval.

Dolbin, under his breath, "All of it liberated from wealthy families, most of them Jewish."

Göring waves to the assemblage like The Savior offering his blessing. "And now we must be off. I expect to see you all in December. *Guten Nacht, guten Nacht.*" Göring takes Emmy by the arm, and they sweep out the door.

Lang gives Dolbin a nudge and smirks, "Keep your eyes peeled that he hasn't made off with some of your drawings under his coat."

Dolbin shrugs, "More likely mine are destined for the burn pile."

Scene 3. A Sitting Room in the Home of Joseph and Magda Goebbels — 1931.

A sitting room that also serves as Goebbels's office. There is a desk with neat stacks of papers arranged on top. To one side, a glass-fronted cabinet holds a collection of kitschy porcelain figurines and a World War I German "iron pot" helmet. Strewn around the floor are children's toys — a wooden rocking horse, a baby doll with blonde hair, some alphabet blocks, and a popgun missing its cork. Hanging at the rear, a poster with a black Swastika on a red background with the words, "Vote National Socialist German Workers' Party."

A doorbell rings insistently. Goebbels enters from the other side of the room and hastens to answer the door, kicking aside toys in his path. He is a thin man in his mid-30s with slicked-back black hair. He walks with a pronounced limp due to a clubfoot. He is the District Leader of Berlin and chief propagandist for the National Socialist Party, later to become Reich Minister of Propaganda.

"Heinrich! Maria! The door! Dammit to Hell, where is everybody? Must I play doorman myself?"

Goebbels disappears into the outer hallway and reappears, followed by Heinz, a tall man in a Brown Shirt uniform. He carries a large, flat package wrapped in brown paper.

"Fresh from the printer, Herr Goebbels. I thought I should deliver it to you myself."

Goebbels seizes the package and tears off the wrapping. It is a poster mirroring the one hanging in the background. He examines it closely.

"Excellent! Excellent!" he exclaims. "Have three thousand of these printed immediately and post them all over Berlin. Make sure you saturate the streets leading to the Reichstag."

"Three thousand? Does the Party have the budget for that many?"

Goebbels pulls himself to his full height and stares into Heinz's eyes. "Herr Hitler has sent us funds from Munich. We must win the vote in Berlin. It's an embarrassment to me that we got so few votes in the last election. We can't be a national party by relying on farmers alone." He pokes a finger into Heinz's chest. "Now, go and see that this is done today!"

Heinz gives him a deep military bow. "I'll oversee the action myself." He gives Goebbels the Nazi salute, does an about-face, and leaves.

Magda Goebbels enters from the back of the house. She is an attractive woman in her early thirties and the mother of, at this point, her first two children. Like her husband, she is highly placed in the National Socialist Party.

"Was that Heinz?" she asks. "I heard the door."

"Yes, he brought the proof for the poster. Where have you been? It's like a tomb in here."

"Let me see." She takes the poster from him and scrutinizes it. "I was upstairs with little Heidi. She has a fever. The nurse is with her."

"Where is Helga? Not here to pick up her toys, I see."

"Nanny took Helga to the zoo. Anna is with her." She hands the poster back to him. "This looks very good, but I would have punched up the red. When do they go up?"

"Today. Heinz is seeing to it."

"Good man, Heinz. Have you seen the paper?"

"I edit the paper."

"I mean, The Red Flag," Magda says.

"That Communist paper? I have people who read it and report to me. Why are you reading it?"

"To see what our people may be missing," she replies. Today, there is to be a rally protesting Paragraph 218. You need to send some men to break it up."

"Two eighteen? The anti-abortion measure? The Reichstag will surely pass it. Who is protesting it?" Goebbels asks. "The Communists?"

"A bunch of rich women whose husbands can't control them," she says bitterly. "Socialists and obviously Jews. We can't have them saying the decision to ban abortion is a criminal act. Germany cannot allow abortion when we need to increase our population as a way to overwhelm our enemies. You said that yourself in your radio speech." She grabs his arm. "Send some men to chase those silly women away. Have some of them arrested as a warning. They'll be gathering at six at Potsdamer Platz."

Goebbels pulls away from her and rushes to the telephone on his desk. "I'll try to phone Walter."

"You must reach him, or I'll go there myself," she demands.

"What, to try and shout down a mob of crazy Jewesses?" He shouts into the phone, "Hello, this is Goebbels. Is Walter there? Well, find him!"

Magda's anger swells. "These women place themselves above the Fatherland. They are selfish and evil. Abortion is a cancerous idea. Look at me, Joseph, I gave you two healthy daughters, with more on the way, I promise you. And they will give birth to dozens of healthy sons. That is our legacy for the Fatherland."

Goebbels finally connects with his enforcer. "Hello, Walter, I need you to take ten, twenty men and get over to Potsdamer Platz before six o'clock…Well, as many as you can assemble…It's the Jews."

Scene 4. A Rally in Berlin's Potsdamer Platz.
As twilight descends, a podium, illuminated by a single spotlight, has been set up on the sidewalk. A crowd made up mostly of women has gathered, spilling out into the street. They chant, "No, no, on Two Eighteen." Thea steps up to the podium and adjusts the microphone. She begins speaking, calmly at first, then with increasing volume and fervor.

"My friends, I concur with the previous speakers against Paragraph 218 of the Criminal Code. Our long-term goal is to find a new form of preventing pregnancy and therefore to make the entire Paragraph 218 unnecessary."

"Immediately, however, the Paragraph must fall because it is no longer morally recognized by women. It is no longer a law. We need a new sexual code because the old one was created by men, and no man is in a position to understand the agony of a woman who is carrying a child she knows she cannot feed."

"This law is derived from male psychology, which forces a woman into having a child. It creates, even if not deliberately, constitutional inferiority of women in relation to men, which serves as a bulwark against women's activity in economic and political life."

"I say we continue to fight and speak out against this law that was put forth by a small number of weak men currently in the Reichstag. They only rule from weakness, but we shall rule through strength!"

Applause erupts, following more chanting of "No, no on Two Eighteen." Thea raises her fist to the sky.

Two Nazi Brown Shirts emerge from the shadows. They rush to the podium and whisk Thea away.

Scene 5. A Bare, Darkened Room in the Offices of the Berlin National Socialist Party.

Thea is sitting at a battered wooden table. One bare light hangs above her. The two Brown Shirts are on either side of her. One perches on the edge of the table, a stein of beer in hand. The other leans against the wall, smoking a cigarette.

"How long am I supposed to wait here?" she asks with an air of contempt.

"Why? Do you need to call your husband?" The Drinker retorts.

"I don't need a husband. I can handle this myself," Thea replies.

"*Ach du Lieber*, she's a feisty one," The Smoker chuckles.

"Like a whore, but a high-class one," The Drinker says.

"One you can't afford," Thea interjects.

The two men laugh, then turn silent.

"Wait, he's coming," The Smoker whispers.

The sound of footsteps, one strong and one dragging, grows louder. Goebbels appears from the darkened hallway. He dismisses the two Brown Shirts and turns to Thea.

"I trust you were treated kindly."

"Joseph Goebbels," Thea says, feigning surprise. "I recognize you from your photo in *Der Angriff*. You are less handsome in person."

Goebbels smiles. "Thank you, I'll take the compliment. And I am happy to hear that you read our paper."

"I read all the papers. It stimulates my thinking."

"Shall I address you as Fräulein von Harbou, or Frau Lang?"

"Von Harbou is my professional name. Lang is private."

"Then I shall keep this professional, Fräulein von Harbou. I am a great fan of your writing, your novels, and films. I particularly liked *Metropolis*. I was taken by your view of the future, a technological paradise, so like what we are working to achieve for Germany."

"The films are a collaboration with my husband."

"So you say, but I can detect your voice in the dialogue, the scenario. I was trained as a philologist, you know," Goebbels adds.

"Philology, the study of words. You do have a way with them, don't you?"

"I have a bit of a literary background, as well," he says with a hint of pride.

"Yes, I read your novel," she says. "The title was Michael, wasn't it?"

"It was. What did you think of it, if I may ask a literary expert?"

"You should go back to literature and give up what you are doing now," she replies.

"Perhaps I shall. Once we have Germany cleaned up, I hope to join our country's literary cadre. But for now, I have other duties."

Thea takes on a sharp tone. "Yes, turning women into robots and forcing subservience to their husbands, taking over businesses for your own profit."

"Only the businesses of Jews and other subversives," he retorts. The Party isn't going to wreck our healthy economic structure. We're not Communists, after all. We look upon the great German companies as partners in a new Fatherland — Krupp, I.G. Farben, BMW, Daimler-Benz, Siemens. And Deutsche Bank, as well, once we flush out the Jews. We appropriate nothing, not even farmland."

He pauses, waiting for Thea to respond. She does not, so he changes topics.

"This new film you are working on, I am told it will be with sound. I am interested in new technologies."

"It will be the first sound film produced in Germany."

"Ah, a 'talkie,' as the Americans call it. I saw The Jazz Singer the year it came out. Tell me about your film."

"It's about children. German Children."

Goebbels waits for her to say more, but she does not.

"Wonderful. We love children, Magda and me. Two little towheads, with more to come. And my wife agrees, in fact, it is her idea to build toward the future of Germany with children. Perhaps when all this mess is cleaned up in three or four years, you will write more films about children. You have a rare gift."

"Thank you. And thank you for sharing your vision," she says. She suppresses a smile, trying to remain aloof.

"My pleasure. I am sure we will talk again, as your talents are of great value to the Fatherland. And now, I suppose you would like to get back to work." He motions for her to stand. "I trust you have had enough of those shrill women. Stay away from them, as they will only tarnish your reputation. You are, after all, a von Harbou. And you come from, let's be clear, an aristocratic family, a pure daughter of the Fatherland."

"Please do not comment on my purity, or lack of same. I leave that to the morning papers," she replies.

"I apologize if you think I have not treated you respectfully.

We are not ogres here."

They stare at each other for a moment until Goebbels breaks the silence.

"Now, I'll have one of my staff drive you home."

"That's kind of you, but I prefer to take a taxi."

"As you wish." Goebbels watches her intently as she leaves the room.

Scene 6. A Street Near Goebbels's Office.

It is now night and raining, and the darkened street is lit by a single streetlamp. As Thea walks briskly through the rain, she tries to hail a taxi but is unsuccessful in both attempts. A figure comes rushing from behind her, carrying an umbrella. He calls for her to wait. It is Ayi.

Thea turns toward him. "What? Ayi, is it you?" She collapses into his arms.

"Yes, I followed you from the rally."

"Oh, my angel," she whispers, "I've had such a time."

They kiss lovingly.

"I saw them take you away, and I followed in a taxi. I've been waiting in the shadows. Another minute, and I was going in after you."

"They let me go. Goebbels himself questioned me — look, I'm trembling. I put on a brave face and said as little as possible. He's terribly clever, almost as if he were trying to court me. He's a villain out of my own novels, a real-life Dr. Mabuse."

"It's good you didn't come in," she adds. "A dark-skinned Communist alien to my rescue — that would have been a scene."

"I'm not a Communist; I just write for their papers."

"That makes you a Communist to them, my sweet."

"But I am an alien and dark skinned."

Thea pulls him closer. "My dark angel, I need to be held."

"Then, I'll hold you."

"Not here, you silly boy, back at my flat."

He flashes her a teasing grin. "But what about Fritz?"

"Fritz," she laughs. My dear, we have three things in our favor. One, he'll be shooting the pursuit scene all night. Two, once he's wrapped, he'll head straight for Lily's place. And three, if he should come home before dawn, you'll run down the back stairs and out through the basement like the sly mongoose you are."

She kisses him. "Now, hail us a taxi. Maybe your male voice will be more successful."

Scene 7. On the Set of *M*.

The set depicts a Berlin street. At one side and to the rear, a flight of stone steps leads to an upper level of the sidewalk. Lang is positioning the actors, Anna, a girl of 12 years, Emil, a boy about 10, and Peter Lorre, who plays Franz Becker, the murderer. A script girl takes notes on a clipboard. Off to one side is a movie camera on a wheeled tripod. At the other side, two canvas folding chairs face toward the set. On the back of one is printed, "Herr Lang," on the other, "Herr Lorre."

The children are dressed in school uniforms. Lorre is in a well-worn business suit, tie, and fedora. Emil is off-camera to the left and holds a red helium-filled balloon on a string. Lorre stands behind Emil, waiting to enter the set. He holds a similar red balloon on a string. Lang finishes his business with the actors and takes his seat in his chair, where he picks up his copy of the script.

Fritz barks a loud command. "Let's begin. Are the lights set?"

"Lights are set," comes a voice from the shadows.

"Roll camera."

"Camera rolling," says the cameraman.

"Roll sound."

"Sound rolling," the sound engineer responds.

"You realize this is an auspicious moment, gentlemen," says Fritz. "We are the first studio in Germany to shoot a sound film."

The script girl rushes forward with the clapperboard and calls, "M, Street Scene 14, Take One." She pushes the two parts of the board together with a loud "thwack," and retreats to pick up her clipboard.

Like an officer ordering "over the top" for his men to charge, Lang calls, "Action!"

Emil skips down the street with his balloon in tow. Anna watches after him and does not see Lorre approaching from behind with a balloon. He is right behind her when he speaks.

"I bet you'd like to have a balloon, too."

Startled, Anna turns toward Lorre. "Yes, yes, I would."

"Cut, cut," Lang interrupts. "Anna, you're too happy. You want the balloon, but you're afraid of him. Remember how we rehearsed it?"

"Let's try it again."

The script girl rushes forward and claps the board again. "*M*, Street Scene 14, Take two."

Once again, Emil skips down the street with his balloon. Anna watches him, and Lorre appears behind her.

"I bet you'd like to have a balloon, too."

Startled, Anna turns toward Lorre. "Yes, yes, I would."

"Cut, cut. Anna, you're still too happy. Take it again."

Once again, the script girl calls, "*M*, Street Scene 14, take three."

Board claps, microphone is placed, and Emil skips down the street. Anna watches him, and Lorre appears behind her.

"I bet you'd like to have a balloon, too." Even with the third take, there is not a trace of frustration in his voice; he is a consummate actor.

Still startled, Anna turns toward Lorre. "Yes, yes, I would."

Lang slams his script on the floor. "Cut, cut, cut, cut. No, that's not what I want, Anna. How many times are you going to do it incorrectly?"

"Fritz, I think she'll be fine," Lorre appeals.

Lang waves Lorre's words away and bends down over Anna. "Do I need to go out and hire another actress who can do two things — be frightened and want the balloon?"

Anna is nearly speechless. "No, Herr Lang."

"I think I may have to."

Anna is at the point of tears. "Oh, no, Herr Lang. Please don't send me away. Please let me try it again. My mother would be devastated. Oh, please."

Lang hastens out of camera range. "Roll camera and sound. This is it."

The script girl hurries forward, now showing signs of nervousness that is sweeping the set. "*M*, Street Scene 14, Take four."

Emil skips, Anna watches, and Lorre comes up from behind.

"I bet you'd like to have a balloon, too."

Startled, Ann turns toward Lorre. This time, she registers both joy and fear. "Yes, I would," she says.

After a pause, Lang calls, "Cut, that was perfect. Anna, you were wonderful."

Lang rushes onto the set, hugs Anna, and plants a kiss atop her head. "I knew you could do it."

Anna brushes away a tear and whispers, "Thank you, Herr Lang."

Lang turns to the crew. "Now then, set up for the chase scene down the staircase. Herr Lorre, we'll start with you."

"I need ten minutes," the sound engineer apologizes. "We blew a tube in the recorder."

"Dammit!" Lang yells. "Can you do it in five?"

Not waiting for an answer, Lang storms off as the sound engineer tears into the tape recorder. The script girl calls a ten-minute break.

Lorre walks over to his chair, followed by Anna and Emil.

"How long do you think we'll have to wait?" Anna asks.

"Not long. Herr Lang is a very persuasive man. The recorder will do as he says."

"I hate waiting," Emil declares. "I'm a man of action."

"You're not a man, you're a boy," Anna says.

"But I'll be a man one day."

"Very true, God willing," agrees Lorre.

"I wish we had something to do," Anna whines. "Peter, you could tell us a story."

"Yes, a scary story," Emil says. "I like scary stories."

"A scary story, eh? Let's see." Lorre pauses to think. He takes longer than he needs, just to build the children's anticipation. "Ah, I think I know one!"

"Tell us, please," Anna says.

"Once upon a time, in a faraway land, there lived a king," Lorre begins.

"Was he a good king?" Emil asks.

"No, not really, because all he did was go to war with all the countries around him. He was very good at war, and his armies were the best. So, when he started a war with his neighbors, his armies were very successful and drove his enemies off the battlefield."

"Then, he was victorious," Emil says, "but that's not scary; it's good."

"But wait," Lorre replies. "This time, victory was within his grasp, but he found that his troops were outnumbered. You see, if he had fought with only one of the enemy countries, he might have won. But he fought with them all at the same time. Then, the rains came, and all of the armies got stuck in the mud."

"Oh, I don't like mud," Anna declares. "I have to clean my boots, and Mother won't help."

"So, after sitting in muddy trenches for a whole year, all the armies gave up the war and went back home."

Emil is disappointed. "The king's army, too?"

"Yes, the king's army went home, too. And the king was terribly embarrassed that he didn't win, so he ran away, never to be seen again."

"Was he eaten by a monster? Emil asks. "If this is going to be a scary story, you'll need a monster."

"Or a wicked witch," Anna adds.

"Wait, wait," Lorre chuckles, "You're getting ahead of me. After the king left, the people of his country fell into dark, dark times. There wasn't enough food. There were no jobs. And the people grew frustrated and angry with one another. They wanted a new king to help them, but they couldn't decide who it should be. They were divided into two groups, one wore red and the other wore brown."

"Did they have machine guns and airplanes to bomb each other?" Emil asks hopefully.

"Even worse," Lorre answers. "Before long, a group of men

decided on a plan. Since they couldn't choose a king, they would make a king themselves — out of mud. It so happened that there was a lot of leftover mud from the trenches the army fought in. So, they gathered some of it and molded a man out of mud. Now, meine Liebchen, here is the scary part. At first, the mud-man was only as big as a baby doll."

Anna turns up her nose. "I wouldn't want a baby doll made out of mud!"

"The next morning, the people discovered that the mud-man had grown to over three meters tall. And he began to speak. 'I am the Golem, and you must obey me. I am hungry, so bring me all the food you can find.'"

"The people saw what they had made out of mud — a monster, a golem, but they were too afraid to say no to him. So, they brought him all the food they could find, and he ate it all in three big gulps."

"The next day, the Golem had grown as tall as a mountain. And he was still hungry, but the people were out of food for him. So, he began to eat the people. Whole fistfuls of men, women, and children — all of them were swallowed up by the Golem. And the Golem grew bigger and bigger, day by day. And so did his appetite for people, until all of them were in the belly of the Golem."

"If the Golem were here, would he eat us, too?" Anna asks, her eyes wide.

"Oh, yes, for his appetite is insatiable."

"What did he do next?" Emil asks.

"People say that he grew sleepy because his belly was so full. And that he moved to the mountains, lay down, and fell asleep. But one day, he will wake up and come down out of the mountains and begin eating again. Me…"

He points to the children in turn. They shriek in delighted terror.

"…and you…and you. Was that scary enough for you? It is for me."

"If the Golem comes again, I'll wash him away with a fire hose," Emil says.

"Very wise, young man. If he comes again, I hope you have a fire hose handy."

The script girl calls to Lang that all are ready to resume shooting.

Lang appears, rubbing his hands in anticipation, "Very good. Peter, I want you at the top of the stairs."

Lorre puts on his fedora and hastens up to the top of the stairs.

The script girl announces to the crew, "Set up for Scene 38, The Pursuit of Beckert. Children, you are excused for the day but tell your parents to have you back here at ten o'clock in the morning."

The children yell, "Yes, ma'am," as they run off to join their parents. The crew repositions the lights and camera for the next shot. Lang calls Lorre down to him, and Lang grabs him by his lapels.

"*Heilige Scheiße*, you're too neat. Remember, Beckert is pursued by a mob. He falls, but he gets up and eludes them. Right now, he pauses for breath. He's panting and disheveled. Go back to the top of the stairs and muss yourself up more. And tighten up, you're too relaxed."

Lorre returns to the top of the stairs. He takes off his hat, musses up his hair, and puts the hat back on at a skewed angle.

"No, no, no," Lang growls, "still not disheveled enough. Now, tighten up. You've fallen and you're in pain. Gertrude, run up there and muss him up some more."

Gertrude, the script girl, runs up the stairs to Lorre. She rips off his hat, throws it on the floor, and stomps on it. She rips out one shirt tail, slaps him across the face, then runs back down to her seat. Lorre retrieves his hat and pulls it down over his ears.

Lang shakes his head in dismay. "That's still not it. There's no panic or pain in your eyes."

"Fritz, I'm an actor. I can do this," Lorre protests. Lang runs up the stairs, grabs Lorre, and throws him down the staircase. Lorre lands in a heap. Lang helps him up and looks him in the eyes. "Good, good. This is what I want. Now, we can start."

Lang resumes his place in the director's chair as Lorre limps back up the stairs.

"At last, we can begin," Lang mutters. "Roll camera, roll sound," he shouts.

Scene 8. Thea and Fritz's Apartment. The Next Morning. Thea is seated on the couch, sipping tea and writing on a pad of paper. Morning sun streams through the curtains behind her. She calls in the direction of the bedroom, "You'd better leave, my dear. It's seven o'clock."

Ayi appears in the bedroom doorway. He is putting on his suit jacket.

"He might show up soon, so let's avoid a scene," she says.

She looks up from her notes. "Better run a comb through your hair." She gets up and walks over to Ayi and adjusts his tie. "Let's straighten you up, you look all rumpled."

"I feel rumpled, but in the best way," he says and pulls her to him for a kiss.

Thea pulls away. "Enough for now, I have work to do. Comb your hair and take the back stairs."

"*Auf Wiedersehen, mein Liebchen,*" he says, pulling her in for another kiss.

Thea shoos him away. "*Auf Wiedersehen, aber gehst du.*"

Ayi blows her a kiss as he exits through the bedroom. Thea returns to the couch and her writing. A moment later, Lang enters noisily through the front door.

"Well, you're up early," he says.

"And you're home late." Without looking up at him, she asks, "Who'd you take to The Green Parrot?"

"It was The Circle."

"Oooh, expensive. I hope she appreciated it."

He waves toward her writing. "What are you doing?"

"We need to start on Dr. Mabuse. You should finish shooting

M in two weeks, and one of us has to think about the next film."

"I can't finish shooting and editing in two weeks; I need more time. I will take more time."

"No, you won't," she says. "Nebenzahl has scheduled the opening for May 1st. By the way, aren't you going to ask me how things went at the rally?"

"Tell me."

"If you don't already know, you must not have been at The Circle to hear the gossip. Quick cut to Lily's apartment, eh?"

"Very well, how did your speech go over?"

"It must have gone over quite well, because just as I finished, the Brown Shirts attacked us, and I was dragged off to see Goebbels at National Socialist Headquarters."

Lang cannot contain his surprise. "Goebbels! What did he say? Did he ask about me?"

"He was more interested in hearing about the technology of sound films. He wants to add sound to the Party's political films." She takes the opportunity to further skewer him. "Perhaps he'll call you about it. Make sure he has Lily's number as well in case you're with her."

"Goebbels can go piss up a rope."

She ignores his response and plunges on. "Herr Goebbels painted a rosy picture of a new Germany. He says that all this unpleasantness will get worse but will last only a few years until Germany emerges reborn and poised to take its rightful place as the leader of Europe. Imagine! The Fatherland as the hub of Western culture!"

Lang glares at her. "You're really taken in by all this *Scheiß*, aren't you?"

"I am a German, aren't I?"

"You certainly are, right down to the von in von Harbou."

"I won't apologize for my lineage. On the other hand —

"Yes," he cuts in, "on the other hand, one branch of my family tree has a Jewish mother hanging from it."

"Don't put words in my mouth. I was about to say that, on the other hand, the true Germans are the ones who put the Fatherland first in their lives. And that includes masses of Germans who are not 'vons'"

"That's a quote from somewhere, isn't it? Perhaps from your new friend Goebbels?"

Thea glares back at him. "You are a bastard! But thank you. You have stirred me up sufficiently to write a monologue for…" She pauses for dramatic effect. "*The Testament of Dr. Mabuse.*"

She turns back to her pad and pencil and begins scribbling furiously.

The Dr. Mabuse character is well-known in Germany, part mad scientist, part gangster, part would-be ruler of the world. This would be Lang and von Harbou's second film featuring Mabuse, who succeeds by guile and the ability to hypnotize and read the minds of others. Some have seen him as a part of "the temper of the times."

Scene 9. A Radio Studio in Berlin. 1933.

Joseph Goebbels sits at a microphone, holding pages of a script. A Brown Shirt wearing earphones stands beside him, looking at his watch and counting down from ten. When he reaches "one," he points to Goebbels and exits quietly. Goebbels begins to read.

"Good evening, fellow members of the National Socialist German Workers' Party and all people of Germany. Tonight, we bring news of historic significance. We have won a great victory at the polls. We have leaped ahead of all the other parties in the Reichstag to where we now have the strongest voice. The Communists, the Socialists, and other Jew-filled and Jew-supported parties must now bend to our will. The Reichstag, our seat of government, is now ours! We will now push forward our agenda to make Germany supreme in Europe and in the world. The way has been paved, the place has been set for us tonight because that great hero and patriot, His Excellency Paul von Hindenberg has named Adolf Hitler Chancellor of Germany! Heil Hitler, and may God bless the Fatherland under his leadership!"

Scene 10. A Sitting Room in the Home of Joseph and Magda Goebbels.
The room is as it was earlier. But now, all the toys have been put away. Magda Goebbels is sitting in a chair, reading a newspaper. A knock at the door, and Magda goes to answer it. Emmy Göring enters.

Magda greets her guest warmly. "Frau Göring, please do come in."

"Thank you, Frau Goebbels, it is so good to see you again." They hug and air kiss.

"Do sit down," Magda says. "I know you wanted to talk before the Grand Ball, but two of the children have been ill, and I haven't been able to get away. It is I who should've come to you."

Emmy sits in a chair opposite Magda. "Think nothing of it. It was easy for me to come over, now with a car and driver, and all. But our home has been a fright since the wedding — and thank you again to you and Herr Goebbels for the lovely silver goblets — but we are in a turmoil rearranging the great hall to accommodate my husband's growing art collection."

"Herr Göring is destined to lead a museum."

"All the museums in Germany, I am told," Emmy responds. "He's got our staff rearranging the present collection. The old masters I'm fond of, but I can't abide the expressionists. Egon Schiele is a fright. I can't stomach his work."

"One of the decadents, I'm sure," Magda agrees. "All that Jewish art should be burned and reduced to ashes."

"If Hermann insists on keeping it, I shall demand that all of it be stored in the basement. It makes me shudder." Emmy executes a stage shudder. "But let's put that aside — I need your advice on the Grand Ball. Specifically, what to wear."

"My advice?" Magda suppresses a laugh. "My dear, you are the actress; it should be me asking for your advice. But let's see — I think that since the Ball is in honor of Herr Hitler and his assumption of the Chancellorship, something festive would be in order —

for us women, of course. The men will be in military uniform or black tie. Herr Goebbels wants a few Party members in Brown Shirt uniforms, but just a sprinkling to make a point. It's a ball, not a rally, after all."

"But the women? You and I?"

"I've given it some thought," Magda says. "We know that Herr Hitler is fond of opera, so I'm thinking about gowns that hint at characters from opera. Festive gowns in bright colors."

"Yes, Italian opera," Emmy says excitedly. "Il Trovatore, Rigoletto. I would choose Gilda from Rigoletto, and your gown should suggest Leonora."

"What about Wagner?" Magda asks.

"My dear, there is nothing festive about Wagner," Emmy retorts. "But I can see Eva Braun echoing Brunhilde, helmet, breastplate, and all." The women laugh heartily.

"Yes," Magda chokes back more laughter. "She is such a country bumpkin. Pure Bavarian."

She suddenly becomes serious. "But he has chosen her, so we must be respectful."

"Do you suppose Fritz Lang will attend?" Emmy muses. "With Thea, of course."

"I suspect not. Since his film about the child murderer — which I found abhorrent — made such a splash, he is shooting another picture that will have sound. Joseph went to Lang's studio last week to look at the recording equipment. Herr Goebbels is eager to add sound to our own films. As for Thea, she wouldn't go alone, and certainly not with her so-called escort."

"Do tell."

Magda pulls her chair closer to Emmy. "She's been seeing this Indian journalist, the one who keeps writing about how Germany should help free India from the British." She picks up the newspaper she has been reading and shows it to Emmy. "Here, look at this."

"Does Herr Lang know about the affair? We all know what a womanizer he is, but when the tables are turned —"

"I've heard they are headed for a divorce. Evidently, there was quite the blow-up."

From outside, a muffled explosion rattles the wall behind them. The two women run to the window and pull aside the drapes.

"Look, down the street," Emmy shouts. "That building is on fire, and the roof has collapsed."

Magda is trembling. "It's the Reichstag. It's the Communists!"

"No," says Emmy, "It's the Jews."

Scene 11. Thea and Fritz's Apartment.
The apartment is empty. Lang bursts through the door, carrying a briefcase. He begins pulling out sheaves of papers, stacking them on the desk.

He shouts toward the bedroom, "I'm back. Power outage in the neighborhood, so we had to wrap. *Gott sei Dank*, we finished the last scene. It's onto the editing tomorrow, so I'll be busy."

Thea appears in the doorway to the bedroom. She wears a

dressing gown and obviously nothing else. At forty-five years of age, she remains the attractive woman she always was. She stares at Lang defiantly.

Fritz is taken aback. "What have you...?"

"I was taking a nap."

"At eight o'clock in the evening? You never nap."

After a moment, Lang realizes the situation and storms into the bedroom. He walks slowly back into the sitting room, followed by a shirtless Ayi.

"Well, there you have it, my dear," Thea says. "Our toboggan ride is over. We hit a tree. I'll spare you the pot-and-kettle speech."

"In my own home?" Lang shouts.

"Technically, it's our home," Thea says, "But you may have it to yourself. I'm moving out until the divorce is finalized."

Lang registers shock. "Divorce?"

"I was going to wait until after you finished shooting the new Dr. Mabuse. But it seems the power outage has short-circuited my plans. I've already filed the papers. Yours should arrive in the morning." She points to the papers Lang has placed on the desk. "You can add them to your stack."

"You'll become a laughingstock throughout Berlin…throughout Germany."

Thea cocks her head and sighs, "Oh, Fritz, listen to yourself. Surely you can't be shocked that I've had enough. You and Lily have been an open secret for years. People will understand, and I'll salvage a bit of self-respect. Don't deny me that."

Lang turns to Ayi. "And what of you? Where do you fit into all this?"

"Thea and I have fallen in love."

"Love? In love? You are nothing but her exotic patchouli-oiled toy." Lang sweeps his arms to indicate the Indian décor. "Just another piece of 'mystic India'," he sneers. "I suppose you two have been practicing the Kama Sutra in my bedroom."

"Ayi, get dressed," Thea commands. "Fritz, go spend an hour at a café. Give us some time to pack a few things, and when you come back, you'll have the place all to yourself."

"You're moving into his place?"

"Oh, horrors, no. You've seen what a dump he lives in." She shouts toward the bedroom, "Sorry, my dear, but you admit it's a pigsty."

She turns to Lang. "As if a Hindu would know anything about pigsties. No, I've taken a flat not far from here. And yes, Ayi will be joining me."

Lang throws up his hands. "Fine. I won't stop you, but you'll regret this."

"Oh, I've been such an idiot," Thea exclaims.

She rushes to the desk and pulls a script from a drawer. She waves the papers in his face. "How could I have forgotten? This is for you, my dear. The finished script for our *Testament of Dr. Mabuse*. I think you can take it from here. Why, it practically directs itself."

She looks toward the ceiling. "*The Testament of Dr. Mabuse*, script by Thea von Harbou, direction by Fritz Lang." She looks at

Lang and whispers, "On the marquee, of course."

Thea hands him the script and pushes him gently toward the door. "Now, go somewhere and have coffee and a nice strudel. Come back in an hour, and we'll be gone."

The phone rings and Lang picks up. "Lang here…When?…Arson? Thank you, I'll tell Thea."

Fritz puts down the phone. "The Reichstag has gone up in flames. They're sure it's arson."

Ayi appears in the doorway. "Now, the blame will begin."

Scene 12. The Radio Broadcast Booth Once Again. Goebbels is seated behind a microphone, script in hand. He reads with gravity and authority.

"People of Germany, we continue to be in a state of emergency since the cowardly attack on the Reichstag, the seat of our government, by the Communists and their collaborators. Therefore, under directives of Chancellor Hitler, the following has been ordered for the protection of the People and the State, effective immediately.

"Articles 114, 115, 117, 118, 123, 124, and 154 of the Constitution of the German Reich are suspended until further notice.

"It is therefore the executive order to restrict the rights of habeas corpus, freedom of expression, including freedom of the press, the freedom to organize and assemble, and the privacy of postal, telegraphic, and telephonic communications. Warrants for house searches will be issued, along with orders for confiscations of the property of subversives.

"The Communist Party is hereby disbanded and its treacherous leaders, including members of Parliament, are being arrested, along with collaborators and dangerous elements of the Jewish community. Also disbanded are all trade unions and other elements in conflict with German corporations and industries.

"Such enemies of the State will be detained until further notice in state prison facilities, including the newly constructed detention facility at Dachau.

"To ensure the safety of the Reich, Chancellor Hitler, as head of the National Socialist Party, is given sole authority to govern, with the National Socialists now filling all key government positions.

"Heil Hitler and may God bless the Fatherland now under his protection and leadership."

Scene 13. The Green Parrot Night Club. Three Months Later. Lang's mistress, Lily Latté, and Dolbin are seated at a table having drinks. They are waiting for Lang to join them. Lily looks at her watch. "He said he was meeting with the censorship board. If it's taking this long, it can't be good. *The Testament of Dr. Mabuse* must be raising eyebrows."

"Perhaps, they want him to make some changes," Dolbin says.

"Fritz would never agree to that," Lily says. "I rather think he's debating with them. But they are such little men. They fear their master, and nothing will persuade them."

Lang comes through the door and strides quickly to their table.

His face reflects both anger and anguish. Lily and Dolbin wait for him to speak. He sinks into a chair next to Lily.

"My news is bad, terrible, in fact. *The Testament of Dr. Mabuse* will not be released in Germany. It has been banned because, they told me, 'It poses a threat to law and order and public safety.'"

Dolbin gives Lang a look of confusion. "But I've heard that it is already being shown in France, Belgium, the Netherlands… probably other countries as well."

"Yes," Lang answers, "the producers smuggled out prints to exhibitors all over Europe." He slams his fist onto the table. "But not in Germany!"

Lily grabs Lang by the arm and pulls him close, murmuring soothing, maternal sounds. Lang calms, then sits erect, straightens his tie, and greets Dolbin warmly, as if nothing had happened.

"Good of you to join us, my friend. Did you bring your sketch-book with you?"

Dolbin sweeps the room with his eyes. "I've given up sketch-ing in public. I feel Dr. Mabuse watching me all the time."

Two Brown Shirts walk by the table and continue into a private dining room. They have had one too many beers. Dolbin watches them warily as Lang motions to the waiter to bring them more drinks.

"But isn't Dr. Mabuse one of Goebbels's favorite characters?" Lily asks. "I suppose he wishes for the power of mass hypnosis."

"There is one silver lining," Lang says. "Thea wrote the Mabuse script. If the film causes any future recriminations, she'll share in them."

Fritz and Lily clink glasses in a toast to this idea. The two Brown Shirts walk back through the club, this time with an equally tipsy woman between them, hanging on their arms. "The Green Parrot seems to be attracting a different clientele these days," Dolbin mutters.

A third Brown Shirt strides over to their table. "Herr Friedrich Christian Anton Lang, aka Fritz Lang?"

"I am he," Lang replies.

The Brown Shirt hands Lang an envelope stamped with an eagle gripping a Swastika, the official symbol of the Nazi Party. He gives Lang the Nazi salute, pivots, and walks away.

Lily cranes her neck to see the envelope. "What is it?"

"We'll soon see," Lang mutters. He opens the envelope, takes out the paper, and reads silently.

Lily squirms, and Dolbin bites his lip.

"Come on, don't keep us in suspense," she pleads.

Lang takes a deep breath. "I am summoned to the offices of the Reich Minister of Public Enlightenment and Propaganda, Joseph Goebbels, at one o'clock in the afternoon."

Lang continues to stare at the letter, looking increasingly worried. "Giving me an entire morning to stew," he sighs.

Scene 14. The Office of Joseph Goebbels, the Next Afternoon. Goebbels is sitting at his desk as an aide ushers Lang in. The aide salutes Goebbels and leaves the room.

Goebbels flashes a toothy smile. "Welcome, Herr Lang. So good of you to come. Please sit down."

Lang warily takes a seat.

"Before we begin," Goebbels says, "I want to thank you for introducing us to the marvels of sound film technology. It is already proving very useful to us, if you've noticed the latest newsreels."

Lang clears his throat and utters a quiet "thank you."

"As you know, I am also greatly impressed with your '*M*' film, but I have one quarrel with it," Goebbels adds. "The ending. Highly inconclusive. The villain should not have gone insane. That was not punishment enough. He ought to have been killed by the fury of an outraged mob." Goebbels leans forward. "For the time being, we shall hold up on allowing the film to be released throughout the Reich. You may discuss it with the writer — which reminds me, please send regards from Magda and me to Fraulein von Harbou when next you see her."

Lang quickly represses a smile. "Thank you, I will."

Goebbels drops his cordial voice. "Let me get to the point here. Herr Hitler is a great admirer of your films, as am I. He loved *Metropolis,* and *Die Nibelungen* made him break down and weep — such a beautiful portrayal of the German spirit. Herr Hitler has spoken to me about you. He said, 'Here is a man who will give us great Nazi films!' Therefore, I am authorized to offer you the leadership of all motion picture production in the Third Reich. You, my good friend, will be our Führer of Film."

Lang pauses for a long moment. "I don't know what to say. I am overwhelmed."

"Just say yes. You are the chosen one."

"I may not qualify for such an office," Lang says. "I don't know if you are aware that my mother, who was born Catholic, had Jewish parents."

"We are aware of your background, but arrangements can be made. It is we who decide who is Jewish and who is not. There is precedent to make you an honorary Aryan, which we will do. Nothing shall stand in the way of your becoming President of the Reichsfilmgruppe."

Lang attempts to parry. "Once again, Herr Minister, I am overwhelmed, and at the same time 'tickled pink' as my mother would say. But I am aware that such an honor brings with it great responsibility." He leans closer to Goebbels. "May I have a day or two to give it my most sincere consideration?"

"I see nothing wrong with that, so long as your answer is yes. You may have twenty-four hours to return to me with your decision."

Goebbels rises and shakes Lang's hand. *"Auf Wiedersehen*, Herr Lang. May I have you driven home?"

"That's very kind of you, but I drove here myself."

Goebbels bows politely. "As you wish."

The aide reappears and escorts Lang out of the office. Goebbels goes to the door and watches them walk down the hall.

Scene 15. Thea and Fritz's Apartment. An Hour Later.

The sitting room is now bare of all adornment. The "Lord of the Dance" hanging, the artifacts, and most of the books are gone. Lang, nearly out of breath, bursts through the door. He runs to the window, pulls a drape aside a few inches, and peers out. Seeing nothing, he runs back to the door and locks it. He grabs a large valise and shoves in some papers from the desk. He takes an urn from a shelf and fishes out a roll of banknotes. As he is stashing the bills, Thea calls from the bedroom.

"Ayi, is that you?"

She appears in the bedroom doorway, carrying her purse and a shopping bag filled with various items. "Fritz, what are you doing in such a rush?" she asks.

"I'm going on a trip and have to catch a train.

"A train? To where?"

"Paris, if you must know. I'm leaving Berlin, leaving Germany. And you should, too. I can make the arrangements. Ayi can fend for himself."

"What's this all about?" she asks. "Lorre and Dolbin have left for Paris, too, but they're Jews…When will you return?"

"I don't know. Perhaps never. I just came back from an audience with Goebbels. He wants me to head the new German Film Ministry. He gave me twenty-four hours to return to him with an answer."

Thea is suddenly incredulous. "And you don't want the job?

This would be the capstone of your career. Think of the possibilities."

Lang steps toward her, growing angry. "I have thought of them, but I don't want to be around to say no to him. He says he is willing to overlook my mother's Jewishness. But if I decline the offer, I would be a cooked goose. Not to mention the end of my creative freedom."

"I suppose Lily is going with you."

"She's already left. Took the night train."

Thea begins to plead. "But you are Germany's greatest film director, and I'm not biting my tongue to say that."

"My mind is made up."

"You are the pinnacle of stubbornness, and you are flushing your career down the toilet."

Lang waves his arms, searching for a rejoinder. "I'm known in America. I'll go there."

"Your English is dreadful."

"I'll get a tutor."

"Yes, a young, well-endowed blonde." They both laugh at the mental picture this presents. "Look, Fritz, I know you too well. You will do what you want. But as for me, I'm staying in Germany."

"With Ayi, of course."

"Yes, with Ayi. We're married now."

Lang is taken aback. "What? When?"

"A month ago. Five weeks."

"Oh, yes, I see," he says bitterly. "An alien marries you to stay in the country. That will sit well with the government — and your career."

"I'll ignore the implication of my husband's motives. As for my career, I'm on firm ground. Goebbels called me back to his office, made me a deal, and I accepted. I will be overseeing all script writing and editing for the film industry."

She pauses to collect herself.

"My dear, I thought you would be part of all this," she pleads.

"You should know me better than to think so," he says.

"Fritz, this current political turmoil won't last forever. It will be over in a few years, and a new Germany will arise, with its arts and culture second to none in the world. That's the Germany I am staying for. We've had our secrets, but this will not be one of them." She reaches into her purse and shows him a Swastika armband.

"Yes, I've joined the Party. It's what I see as my duty to the Fatherland."

"You are mad!"

"I love my country," she says, "Not for what it is now, but for what it will become."

"And I shudder to think of what it will become," says Lang, his voice trembling.

He picks up his valise and steps to the door. "Goodbye, Thea. *Bon chance und viel Glück.*"

Thea watches him close the door behind him. "*Danke und auf Wiedersehen, mein Liebchen,*" she whispers.

Epilogue – 1945 and Beyond

Our story of Thea and Fritz doesn't end here; it merely stops in the summer of 1933. You don't need to be a student of history to know that everything gets worse from there on out: the War, the Holocaust, and countless casualties on both sides. We would be remiss if we didn't let you know what happens to these characters in the following years.

First, a person who is never seen in the story, but whose presence permeates the whole. Realizing that the jig was up, Adolf Hitler took his pistol and shot himself to death in his Berlin bunker on April 30, 1945. He was 56 years old. At his side was his long-time mistress and wife of one day, Eva Braun. As Adolf fired the fatal shot into his own head, Eva bit into a cyanide capsule and died alongside him. She was 33.

Later that day, and also in the bunker, Joseph and Magda Goebbels persuaded Hitler's dentist to administer morphine to their six children to put them to sleep. The two parents then placed a cyanide capsule into the mouth of each child, killing them. Joseph and Magda walked outside and used a pistol to commit suicide. He was 47, she was 43.

Hermann Göring was tried at Nuremberg and found guilty of war crimes. He was sentenced to be hanged. But on October 15, 1946, the night before the scheduled execution, someone smuggled him a cyanide capsule, and he took his own life. He was 53.

The former actress Emmy Göring was convicted of being a

Nazi and sentenced to a year in jail. When she was released, she was banned from the stage for five years. In 1972, she wrote a memoir, *My Life with Goering*. She died the next year at age 80.

Benedict Dolbin fled Germany and ended up in New York City, where he wrote reviews for various left-wing publications and became a well-known dance critic. He died in 1971 at age 88.

The actor Peter Lorre escaped Germany in 1933 and moved to Hollywood, where he had a long career in the movies. He is arguably best known for his role in *The Maltese Falcon*, with Humphrey Bogart.

Ayi Tendulkar and Thea von Harbou soon divorced. Ayi returned to India as an activist working with Gandhi to free India from British rule.

The German actress Lily Latté starred in the 1934 film Liliom, the only one Lang made in France. She moved to Hollywood shortly afterward and, fully aware of Lang's endless indiscretions, she nevertheless married him. They were together until the end of his life. Lily died in 1984 at the age of 85.

Fritz Lang moved to Hollywood in 1934 and became one of the era's great directors. He was a major influence on what came to be called film noir, with films like *The Big Heat*, remembered for the scene in which Lee Marvin throws scalding-hot coffee in Gloria Grahame's face. (So very Lang.) Lang directed most of the major stars in Hollywood, including Henry Fonda, who, allegedly, detested him. Peter Lorre, whom Lang threw down a flight of stairs in *M*, never warmed up to him. In all, Lang directed some thirty films in Hollywood. His legacy includes two of the Top 100 Films of all time, *Metropolis*, and *M*. Lang died in Los Angeles in 1976 at the age of 85.

Thea von Harbou authored over a dozen novels and scores of screenplays. She worked throughout the 30s and 40s doing what she loved, writing and editing films. She also got her chance to direct —*Hanneles Himmelfahrt* (Hannele's Journey to Heaven) — a sentimental film meant to boost morale on the home front. At the war's end, von Harbou spent four months in a British prison camp. She denied having any Nazi sympathies and claimed to have only joined the Nazi Party to help Indian immigrants in Germany. Lang's biographer, Patrick McGilligan, wrote: "Her direct work on behalf of the government consisted, she claimed, entirely of volunteer welding, making hearing aids, and emergency medical care. In fact, she received a medal of merit for saving people in two air raids."

Perhaps, she felt a need for atonement. In 1946, she was one of hundreds of "rubble women" who wielded shovels and wheelbarrows to help clean up the devastation of a bombed-out Berlin. She continued to write until her death in 1954 at age 65. In 1959, Fritz Lang returned to Germany to direct *The Indian Tomb*, based on one of von Harbou's novels.

Finally, The Golem. He is always around.

AUTHOR'S NOTES

Thea von Harbou is pronounced "TAY-uh fon HAR-boo."

Ayi is pronounced AY-uh.

Lily Latté is pronounced "Lily La-TAY."

The incident in which Lang throws Peter Lorre down the stairs actually did happen, according to several sources.

Lang has told the story of his final meeting with Goebbels countless times, often with variations. The encounter in this story is based on my own interview with Lang in Austin, Texas, in 1972.

The person who was ultimately placed in the position of President of the Reichsfilm Group, the position Lang refused, was the filmmaker Leni Riefenstahl, who, in 1936, would direct the infamous paean to Nazi power and glory, *Triumph of the Will*.

While in the British prison camp, von Harbou directed a production of *Faust*. The irony seems almost overwhelming.

PHOTOS

Thea von Harbou in an undated photo. Credit Getty Images.

Fritz Lang speaking at the University of Texas at Austin in 1972. From the author's personal collection.

Fritz Lang and Thea von Harbou at work in their Berlin apartment in 1923. AR-CHIVIO GBB/Alamay.

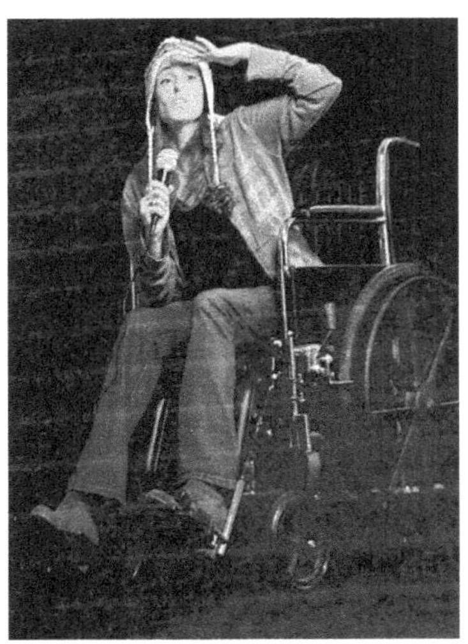

Ann Baker as Jenny in a stage version of Jenny Gets Her Wheels On. Produced by Onstage Theater, Martinez, CA. Directed by Kim Doppe. Photo by Julie Cheshire. Photo owned by the author.

AUTHOR'S BIOGRAPHY

Gary Carr is an author and playwright. Published work includes a book on one of the blacklisted "Hollywood Ten," *The Screenwriting of John Howard Lawson*, published by UMI Press, Ann Arbor, and a collection of short fiction, *The Girl Who Founded Nebraska*, published by EXIT Press, San Francisco. Recent plays include *Love in the Time of Covid*, a comedy about a family trying to live together during the plague, and *Phillis Wheatley: The Poet Who Wrote Her Way Out of Slavery*, about the 18th-century American writer. Many of his essays and short stories have appeared in print and online magazines, including *History Through Fiction, The Journal of Irreproducible Results, Lightwood, Callboard, The New Fillmore, Big Pagoda,* and *The Metaworker*. His plays and screenplays have been produced in California and Texas, several of which have won awards.

He has been a university teacher, co-owner of a film production company, co-owner of a comedy club, corporate communications director, and publicist. He holds a B.A. from Carleton College, an M.A. from Ohio University, and a Ph.D. in Radio-TV-Film from the University of Texas at Austin. Before moving from California to Texas in 2022 with his late wife, Kathy, he was the owner of a San Francisco Bay Area publicity firm that specialized in arts and entertainment. He lives in Gunter, Texas. carrpool@pacbell.net